Tricentennial

IE Castellano

Laurel
Highlands
Publishing

Tricentennial
Second Edition Copyright © 2014 IE Castellano
Original Copyright © 2012 IE Castellano
Rights reserved.

Cover by JosDCreations
http://JosDCreations.com

Laurel Highlands Publishing
Mount Pleasant, PA
USA

http://LaurelHighlandsPublishing.com

ISBN-13: 978-1-941087-18-3
ISBN-10: 1941087183

This book is a work of fiction. Names, characters, places, and
incidents either are products of the author's imagination or are used
fictitiously. Any resemblance to actual persons, living or dead,
events, or locales is entirely coincidental.

For all who preserve
life,
liberty,
and pursue
the happiness for which we all strive.

Chapter 1

Sometimes, I wished my life were different. Especially when I was sitting on the ground, in the middle of nowhere, cold, wet, and hungry. Two days on the run without sleep or food made me long for the comforts that I was used to having.

I grew up in what was called Pod City one-five. It was the only civilized place for hundreds of miles. Civilized meaning technology ruled our lives. Nanotechnology to be specific. Nanotech was incorporated into every aspect of our lives, from our homes, to our devices, to even our clothing.

PC one-five felt like a paradise. My mom, dad, younger sister, and I lived in a comfortable condo pod that housed twelve condos on three floors. We lived on the middle floor. Our corner condo had the best view of the central common area of the city. Some days, I would sit on the couch, watching the pod cars pass on the rails below while wondering where the people inside were going. I could not have asked for more.

Sitting on the cold, soggy ground, I wanted for more. I wanted for my mom, my dad, my jacket, cover from the rain, anything. All I had was my sister. She shared in my misery.

My sister, Nickie, was the reason I was missing my warm, dry, home with a fridge filled with food. Because of her urge to run through no man's land, we were trying to stay one step ahead of the Pod City Protector Units. She insisted it was Dad's idea, but somehow I did not think that he had evading the authorities in mind. Although I could not blame her entirely, I did agree to go along with her plan. Like her, I needed to hold onto something. Dad's vague words were better than nothing, I supposed.

All I wanted was to return to the better times. Like when we would go for a picnic in the reclaimed wilderness outside the electrified fence that surrounded PC one-five. Mom always filled the picnic basket with our favorites, while Dad always made us leave our scrollpads at home.

My entire life was on my scrollpad, which rolled tightly to fit in my pocket. I, of course, had all my class notes, school assignments and friend connections on it. But, I also had found a way to access information anywhere in PC one-five. Because of my early, and more clumsy, attempts at hardwiring my scrollpad to the condo pod's main electrical connection, the Electric Commission visited our condo a couple of times.

The morning of our last family picnic, I had hardwired my scrollpad to the condo's main system. My back door created a skeleton key so I finally had access to the entire Electric Commission. When I had accidentally dimmed the lights in the condo, Mom yelled at me.

"Xavier Kelton," she said in that voice that sent shivers down my spine, "I hope you aren't looking for another visit from the Electric Commission."

"No, Mom," I said. I knew that too many visits from any of the national commissions resulted in dire consequences.

Nickie knocked on my bedroom door. "Dad says that it's time to go," she said.

Leaving my scrollpad, I walked out of my bedroom into the great room. Our condo was one big open room with our bedrooms off of it. Any point in the great room had a calming view of the commons. Mom had the packed picnic basket waiting on the counter. Dad rummaged through a drawer in the kitchen while Nickie and I threw on our jackets.

Everyone in PC one-five wore these jackets. Made of recycled plastic, which gave the coats a blue hue, they were imbued with nanotechnology. The nanotechnology would adjust the fibers in the material to keep people warmer when it was cold and cooler when it was hot. My dad worked for the Nanotechnology Commission. As a sub-atomic scientist, his research helped to breakdown plastic in the recycling process. He explained how his work helped to make the fibers in our jackets as well as all other woven material.

As I stood, waiting to get out into the late summer day, Dad came over with a small knife.

"Caleb?" Mom said confused. She knew knives were prohibited outside of the condos.

3

"We're almost ready to go, Sadie," Dad said with a smile. With the blade in his hand, he walked behind each of us, slicing a two centimeter incision into the left sleeve of our jackets just below our elbows. Wiping off the blade, he returned it to the drawer. "Let's go," he said cheerfully while he picked up the picnic basket.

Mom carried the blanket out of the condo. Nickie and I followed our parents to the waiting pod car. The door slid open with a push of a button. When we stepped inside, Dad placed the basket on the floor of the car. I sat near the window as Dad swiped his Identification Card on the dashboard. After entering our destination into the touch pad, the pod car entered the track system.

The ride from our condo to the gate was weird. Dad made forced small talk. "I hope you packed enough baked chicken," he said to Mom. "I'm starving. Are you kids hungry?" he added along with more stupid stuff. I figured he was waiting to talk about his breakthrough research at the picnic area.

A few nights before that picnic, I awoke thirsty. While I was getting something to drink in the kitchen, I overheard Mom and Dad whispering in their bedroom. "Something is happening to the molecular structure," Dad whispered.

"On its own?" Mom asked.

"Yes. I think it has developed carbon bonds," Dad said. "I would like your opinion, Sadie." Mom was a molecular biologist for the Biotech Commission. Over the years, she had been recognized as a leading expert in dynamic molecular structures.

When our pod car arrived at the gate, Mom and Dad plastered smiles on their faces. The line to go outside the electric fence was considerably smaller than usual. While we swiped our IDs to get through the rotating metal bars, the watching guard smiled at us.

"It's a beautiful day for a picnic, Mister Kelton," he said to my dad. "Seems as if a lot of people have been scared away from the wilderness because of the many attacks."

"Seems like it," my dad responded. All over the news, they were warning people about wild animal attacks. Dad was not concerned about the attacks.

Outside the gate, we moseyed to our usual picnic spot. Mom gave us one of her history lessons. "It still amazes me that this area is only twenty years old," she said. "Of course the planting of older trees helped the reforestation effort." She sighed with sadness.

Mom told us how the area used to be a suburb of the city that spanned across the rivers and into the hills. In school, we learned how even the suburbs were overcrowded. Urban sprawl caused deforestation, which led to animals losing their homes. Concrete covered most of the green areas. The streets and buildings were dirty. It sounded awful when the teacher told it, but Mom always made it sound like a more romantic time that she missed dearly.

She and Dad survived the great plague that killed millions across the country. They remembered a time when buildings reached into the sky. When people drove cars themselves on roads. Life was dirtier then. Mom told us that plague survivors were brought to the quarantine complex. That's where she met Dad. She told us that they spent their first dates watching the city burn out of the complex's window.

As I sat on the soggy ground, remembering a better time, I missed my parents. Mom's stories seemed so trivial that weekend. Truth was, I would have given anything to have been able to hear her stories.

"I think we should keep moving, Xav," Nickie said. She looked terrible with her light brown hair plastered to her head. Red puffiness under her eyes joined the dark circles.

"Do you think they are coming?" I asked.

"I think we should keep going east," she said with a concerned knowing in her eyes.

"How do you we know which way is east?" It had been night for a long while.

Through the darkness, I still saw her roll her blue eyes. "Stop being a baby," she told me. "We can't go back, you know."

"I don't want to go back," I said. There was nothing back there for me. Not even my jacket—it swam with the river currents.

"Good," she said. "Let's go."

Nickie pulled me off the ground. We had been running for two days. Eventually, we slowed to a brisk walk. All I wanted to do was sleep, but it was hard to sleep when you were constantly looking over your shoulder.

I lamented leaving my relatively dry spot. Although I did not think she really knew where we were going, I followed her anyway. Before that moment, we had never been that far from PC one-five. I expected to come across more wilderness like what was closer to the city with lush forest. However, all I saw were overgrown fields and sparse trees. No bears or large cats either, like people had reported seeing while they rode on the magnet rails. We only came across rabbits, squirrels and deer.

Emerging from the tall, wet grass I quietly called, "Nickie!" I squatted to feel a cool, hard, black surface. "What is this?"

"It's a road!" Nickie said. Squinting through the rain, she continued, "A big road. Look!" She pointed in front of us. "A grassy separation, then more road."

I had only seen roads on videos in school. "These must be like the ones Mom and Dad would talk about," I said excitedly. After looking at Nickie, I wished that I could have stuffed those words back into my mouth.

Tears fell uncontrollably from her eyes. She tried to stifle a horrible wailing sound.

Standing, I hugged her wet body. "I miss them, too," I comforted. After she caught her breath, I suggested that we kept walking.

Nodding, she led me across the expansive road. I could barely make out the cracked black road with its faded white and yellow paint under my feet. Nickie froze halfway across the road. "Someone's coming," she said in hushed tones. "We need to hide."

Hearing strange noises, I grabbed her hand. As I pulled her into the trees, my heart beat wildly. We hid inside a large, overgrown bush. I saw fear in her light eyes. My chest pounded while my mind hoped that they—the Pod City Protector Units—had not found us. The noises got closer. Not being able to see anything, I figured they had us surrounded. What was to become of us, if we were caught?

I did not care what happened to me, but I knew they would destroy my sister's independent spirit. Nickie hassled the teachers so much with her questions that eventually Mom had to talk to her. Mom was afraid that if she continued to ask, they would call them unfit parents and take Nickie away.

"Xav," whispered Nickie as she hit my arm.

"What?"

"Look."

Opening my eyes, I peeked through the dense branches. Horses pulled a wagon along the remnants of the old road. On the top of the wagon sat, "A person," I said, "outside the pod cities."

"I know," Nickie said excitedly. "Other people survived the plague. We're not alone out here."

"Nickie," I began. The rain still fell on our heads. I could see hope and excitement in her eyes. "We don't know if these people are plague free or not. There might only be a couple of people." I did not want to completely crush her excitement, but someone had to inject a shred of logic.

"So?" Nickie said defiantly. "This means we've been told wrong. After all we've been taught, year after year, I expected to come across more wild animals like bears and big cats. But, we haven't. They were wrong, Xav."

Those words, *they were wrong*, scared me the most. What else were we taught that was wrong? We were completely unprepared for what was out there. "Nick, how do we know that these people are not behind the attacks we were warned about?" I asked.

"We have to take our chances," Nickie said. "It is what *they* wanted."

Chapter 2

As I followed her out of our hiding place, I kept thinking that maybe they forgot to tell us something.

That last picnic was where Nickie believed our parents gave us instructions. After we ate, Dad brought us to the riverbank. I had never seen Dad look so serious.

"The less you kids know, the better," Dad said.

We had to lean in close to hear him over the sound of the water.

"Life might be changing soon for all of us." He looked down, then out at the river. "The jackets return to the river. Offer them well." Gazing away from the river, towards the wilderness, he continued, "Grandma lived in a big, white farmhouse. You kids should have seen it. It was the best house."

Dad smiled as we returned to our picnic blanket. I was not

sure if he had lost his mind or not. When we returned to our condo, no one spoke of what happened on the riverbank.

Lost in my thoughts, I walked into Nickie. "Why did you stop?" I asked her.

Saying nothing, she pointed.

My eyes followed the line of her finger to a large building in the distance. "Is that a farmhouse?" I asked.

"I don't know," she said, "but it's large and white."

In the darkness, the building looked white-ish. "You think it is the same one?"

Nickie looked at me with her wild look. "Let's check it out," she suggested.

"What if the Protector Units find us?"

"Do you really think they are looking for us?" she asked with one eyebrow raised.

I hoped the answer was no, but after all that had happened, I could not be too optimistic.

Before I could protest, she made a beeline for the house. I tried to catch up to her. She paused at a small overgrown road allowing me to reach her side. I knew what she was thinking. She wanted to feel close to our parents. I could not blame her. That was what I wanted, too. Someone to protect us. Someone to comfort us. Someone to tell us everything would be all right.

"Where are you going?" I yelled in a whisper as my sister crossed the road. Reluctantly, I followed. When she walked up the stairs, they creaked with each step. "Someone could be in there," I warned.

"It's empty," she said, peeking in a window.

Trying to avoid the creaks, I joined her on the porch. "It's peeling," I said as I looked at the dirty white building.

She turned the doorknob, opening the door. A stale smell escaped the house.

"Nickie."

"We haven't slept in days," she said. "I'd rather get out of the rain. Wouldn't you?"

I was so tired that I just agreed with her. Walking inside, she closed the door behind us. The house was dark and smelled like... old, if old had a smell. I followed her into one of the rooms of the creaking house. Two couches faced an empty wall as if a screen hung on it at one time.

Nickie picked the smaller of the two couches, leaving the larger one for me. It felt so good to stretch my legs. Despite the smell and the dust, the back cushion was very comfortable.

My eyes opened while thunder rumbled around the old house. A flash of lightening illuminated the dark room. Nickie slept through the storm on the other couch. I remembered how wildly it stormed that day they called us out of class.

"Xavier Kelton, Nicole Kelton, please come to the office," the woman's voice announced over the loud speaker. Gathering my scrollpad, I joined Nickie in the hall.

"Why do you think they called us?" she asked me.

I simply shrugged my shoulders and kept walking. I could not think of anything that I had done.

When we entered the school office, the lady at the desk walked through a door, saying, "The Kelton kids are here."

Mister Philipps, the principal of the high school, walked out of his office to greet us. "Come in, Xavier, Nicole," he said.

We walked into his office, still wondering why we were

there. He gestured for us to sit in the chairs in front of his desk. When we sat, he did not sit on the comfortable looking chair behind his large desk. Instead, he leaned against his desk, carelessly pushing his picture frame into his touchpad.

"You are probably wondering why you are here," Mister Philipps said. He looked at us kindly before continuing, "Neither one of you are in trouble." He fidgeted with his hands. "There has been an accident at the lab where your father works."

Nickie's face dropped.

"I don't know his condition. Your mother is coming to get you," he said. "Get what you need from your lockers and come back to the office to wait for your mother." His words were a million miles from my ear.

The look on my mother's face when she entered the office was burned into my memory. Her light eyes got lost in her moist lashes and puffy, red face.

"Mom?" said Nickie quietly.

Mom hugged us like we were going to be ripped out of her grasp at any second.

"Missus Kelton," said Mister Philipps. He could not finish his sentence.

"Thank you for my children," Mom managed to say before ushering us out of the school.

"Where are we going?" Nickie asked.

"Home," Mom said.

"Is Dad okay?" I asked.

"We don't know yet," she said as she swiped her ID card in a pod car.

We rode in silence to our condo pod. When we stepped out

of the elevator, a man in a black suit waited in front of our door.

"Sadie Kelton?" he said.

Mom nodded her head.

"May I come inside?" he asked.

She swiped her card in the lock. Opening the door, she nudged Nickie and me inside before letting the man in the black suit into the condo. When she closed the door, she turned to the man then said, "Well?"

He stood just inside the door emotionless. "We at the Nano-techology Commission are very sorry for your loss," he stated.

"I want to bury my husband," Mom said almost defiantly.

The man blinked. "I am afraid that will not be possible," he said.

"I have the option of a burial," Mom argued.

A part of him looked briefly shaken before he said, "Yes, ma'am, you do, but no body was found. Just portions of his DNA."

"Then I'll bury the portions of his DNA," Mom said angrily.

"A grief counselor will be deployed to you," he said. "Arrangements will be made then." He promptly left the three of us alone in our condo.

"No!" screamed Nickie with tears streaming down her face. "No! He can't be dead! He can't be! We just saw him this morning. They just can't find him. He'll come home from work like he always does."

Mom tried to comfort Nickie the best she could. Nickie's cries carried through the condo as we tried to sleep that first night without Dad.

In the days that followed, Mom talked to no one but Nickie

and me. She talked about how she would have liked to have seen Dad's family farmhouse. Since they met during the quarantine, neither Mom nor Dad met each other's families. Mom repeated stories from both her family's past and what she could remember of Dad's family's past. It was as if she did not want us to forget them.

Mom did not talk to the grief counselor they sent either. Sitting the woman on a couch, Mom said, "The kids need you more," then walked away.

The woman was nice enough, but a complete waste of time. Nickie would ignore her whenever she tried to talk to her. I barely heard what she said about how losing a parent was common in his line of work. Mostly, everything that reached my ears sounded like blah, blah, blah.

Dad's funeral did nothing to comfort any of us. All Nickie did was cry uncontrollably. Although shaky, Mom stayed composed. She somberly, yet graciously, accepted condolences. I was impressed with Mom's strength. A part of me hoped that Nickie had inherited some portion of that strength.

After the funeral, life had a new definition of normal. Every morning, Mom would say good-bye as if she thought she would never see us again. After school, as we would wait for Mom to come home from work, Nickie mainly stared out the window into the city commons. Sometimes, she would prepare dinner to alleviate Mom's burden. I spent my time enhancing the condo's appliances and subsequent electrical system, trying to fix things.

The lightning flashed through the window of the old house. Momentary brightness allowed me to watch Nickie sleep. I was glad that she could finally sleep even if it were only from exhaustion.

As the rain lashed the windows, I remembered how badly I wanted it to rain the last time Nickie answered the door of our condo.

Mom was not due to be home for another hour. I kept to my room while Nickie started dinner. From my room, I heard the doorbell. About twenty seconds later, I heard Nickie scream, "No!" then loud footsteps. Emerging from my room, I saw the open door partially covering a woman in a black suit standing on the other side of the door.

When I opened the door fully, the woman said, "Xavier Kelton?"

I nodded my head.

"I am from the Biotech Commission," she stated, looking flat and emotionless.

My stomach dropped because I knew what was coming next.

"Your mother, Sadie Kelton, perished in a laboratory fire," she told me. Whatever she said next never reached my ears.

I could say nothing to her. She walked away, leaving me standing in the open doorway.

A couple of hours later, the same grief counselor as before sat in our great room. Her face was soft with concern and her eyes were warmer than a couple of weeks prior.

"Losing both of your parents within a couple of weeks of each other isn't fair," she said. "You've barely gotten over the loss of your father. And here it is, all over again." She wiped the corner of her eye. "You two are older orphans. I am going to recommend that you stay here until after the funeral."

"And then what?" I managed to ask.

"With your good grades, Xavier, you will report to Pod City Protection a year earlier than usual. You will be assigned to a Protector Unit and then assessed further for employment development." She paused to check her scrollpad. "Unfortunately, you have no living relatives. That means that Nicole will go to live in a group home until she is eighteen."

"Can't I take her when I turn eighteen?"

Closing her eyes, the woman shook her head. "I'm sorry but you will be ineligible to adopt your sister until your development is over. By the time your four years are up, Nicole will already be eighteen."

"But," I said. Nothing else could escape my lips.

Nickie slid down on the couch next to me. I grabbed her hand.

Squeezing my hand, she said, "It will be okay, Xav."

With tears looming in her eyes, she looked at the woman sitting across from us. "Ma'am," she said softly, "before our family erodes completely, would you grant us permission to leave the city for one last picnic?" Tears started to fall down her cheeks. "Our parents took us every," she could not finish.

"Nickie," I said as I put my arm around her.

"It, it would be our way to remember them," Nickie sobbed before covering her face with her hands.

Chapter 3

The woman's face softened even more. I thought she would start crying at any time. "Of course," she said. "A tree can even be planted for them, if you'd like."

Removing her hands from her face, Nickie nodded.

Thunder shook the old wooden monstrosity of a house, bringing me back to the stale smelling couch on which I laid. Being out of the rain was a welcomed change, although I wished I were warm as well.

The sun beat down on our heads as Nickie and I stood around a hole in the ground. People we did not really know surrounded us. The enclosing sadness weighed heavier than at Dad's funeral.

I barely looked at the enrobed man who droned, "We commit the body of Sadie Kelton to the ground." They lowered a coffin into the gaping hole.

"Who's he kidding?" Nickie muttered under her breath.

I gave Nickie a reproachful look. I could not believe that she was being so cavalier.

"At least Mom's empty coffin will rest next to Dad's empty coffin," she said just loud enough for me to hear. Throwing her flower on top of the lowered coffin, she walked through the surrounding people away from the double grave marker with our parents' names.

I glanced momentarily at the resin plaque that said, "Beloved wife and mother," under my mother's name before following Nickie.

"Mister Kelton," the grief counselor called.

It was strange to be called mister. That was what people called my dad. I walked over to where the woman was standing.

"Nicole is lucky to have such a caring brother," she said with obvious redness around her eyes. "I have authorized your pass through the fence for tomorrow. All you'll need to do is swipe your IDs. An oak has been planted in your parents' names."

"Thank you," I said. Not being able to muster anymore, I ran to Nickie's side. When I told her about our picnic for the following day, I saw a wild glint that never had previously visited her blue eyes.

The air in the condo had a funny vibe the morning after Mom's funeral. Our things were all ready for going our separate ways. Nickie packed the picnic basket with leftovers and whatever bottles of juice and nutrition bars we had left in the kitchen cupboards.

Carrying the picnic basket the way Dad did gave me a sick

feeling of loss in my stomach. I watched Nickie hug the blanket down to the waiting pod car. Finality fixated in my mind as I swiped my card to make our last journey together to the gate.

Quietness filled the pod car. Nickie sat in her seat, holding on desperately to the blanket while staring out the window. I had never felt so empty before. A journey outside the electric fence, I thought, would do me some much needed good.

The Protector at the gate recognized us. "I heard about what happened to your folks," he said. "I'm so sorry. They were nice people."

All I could do was nod as I tried to hold back any liquid attempting to escape my tear ducts. Sadness engulfed me. I did not know how I would be able to walk through the gate let alone eat or drink. Luckily, the sun hitting the top of Nickie's light brown head distracted me enough to follow her mindlessly.

By the time Nickie carefully spread the blanket on the ground, numbness fought back the sadness. As I sat on the blanket, like I had numerous times before, its softness did not reach my hands. It was as if the blanket was not beneath me. I had no reason to sit on a blanket I could not feel.

"Wanna see the tree?" I asked.

"Not yet," Nickie said with her arm deep inside the picnic basket. She handed me a bottle of drink and a plastic container of leftover something-or-other. "After we eat."

It felt good to not have to think. I just followed Nickie's lead. She ate; therefore I ate, although my mouth had no idea what it was chewing. My taste buds discerned nothing. I washed my chewed food down with what the bottle said was fruit juice. I could have been drinking water and I would have had no idea.

Taking the empty plastic container from me, Nickie placed both mine and hers back inside the basket. "Okay," she said, "I'm ready to see the tree."

I was not sure if I really wanted to see the tree or not, but I went anyway.

We walked down a paved path that I had never walked down before, which led to the tree plantings. A forest of different aged trees all had dark brown plaques in front of them. Until that moment, I never realized how many people had been remembered just by our little Pod City in only twenty years.

Stopping next to Nickie, I saw a young oak with an engraved dark brown plastic plaque on a plastic pole sitting in front of it. The white lettering read, "In loving memory of Caleb and Sadie Kelton—20 NE."

We stood for a while in silence, staring at the letters and the leaves. The green oak leaves rustled in the light breeze that wound through the remembrance forest. As the breeze caressed my body, it was as if my parents were thanking us for taking the time to have a final family picnic.

"That's nice," Nickie said with her hand touching the leaves. After a moment of silence, she took a deep breath. "Let's go."

We followed the path back to the blanket. In more silence, we drank more juice and munched nutrition bars.

Nickie rubbed the blanket as if she were saying good-bye, then said, "Are you ready?"

"To go?" I asked.

"For a walk," she answered.

Getting up, I followed Nickie down the familiar path that we used to walk with our parents every weekend. The sound of rushing water began to reach my ears.

"Could you imagine people living here?" Nickie said, looking at the tree covered hillside. "Houses made of wood instead of reinforced plastic. Windows made from real glass. Maybe a building of red brick." She had a smile on her face like Mom used to have when she would tell her stories of yesteryear.

I did not bother to burst her bubble with tales of how dirty the hillside used to be. Of how no one could drink the water or breathe the air. Or that litter cluttered the streets and garbage overflowed from the dumps. That the very fact that a neighborhood covered the hill and dominated the surrounding hills helped the plague spread. I could not extinguish the sparkling light in her blue eyes. I just followed her down to the riverbank.

A crack of lightning brought my mind back to the musty house. Looking around the room, I saw Nickie's opened eyes looking at me.

"Do you hear something?" she whispered from the other couch.

"It's just the storm," I whispered back. "Go back to sleep."

In the darkness, I watched her slide off the couch. Crawling over to me, she said, "I think someone is in here."

Listening carefully, I tried to block out the howling wind and rumbles of thunder. Dull thumps reached my ears. My whole body froze. Then, I heard a loud squeak and the distinctive click of a door latch. Quickly, I slid off the couch, joining Nickie on the floor.

"It's the middle of the night," a woman's voice said.

"I don't care what time it is," replied another woman. "You

didn't have to come with me."

"Of course I did," the first woman said. "Wouldn't have heard the end of it."

Looking into the hallway, Nickie eyes opened wide. "Move," she mouthed.

We crawled around to the side of the couch.

"Where do you think it is?" the first woman asked.

"Could be anywhere," the second replied.

My heart beat rapidly out of my chest. I heard the two women's feet move through the house. We scooched around the stale smelling furniture to avoid being seen.

"Mazie," the first woman called.

"What, Char?" Mazie called back. Their voices came from different parts of the house.

"Found something that might interest you," Char said.

The direction of the footsteps was unclear. I could not tell if the women were walking towards or away from us. Looking at Nickie, I tried to get some idea, but she was just as confused as I.

We held our breath trying not to make a sound. The storm even stayed silent for a while. In a flash of lightning, Nickie's face showed a look of abject horror. Her eyes stared over my head. Slowly, I looked behind me.

Chapter 4

In the relative darkness, a woman with a hard look on her face loomed over me. "Well, well, well. Looks like we got ourselves a couple of squatters, Char."

I swallowed hard. Two hard clicking sounds reached my ears.

"Shotgun's loaded," Char said from somewhere behind Nickie.

I had no idea what a shotgun was, but instinct told me that it was not good.

The woman raised a jar containing light above our heads. The jar illuminated her thin lips and lines around her eyes. She reminded me of my dad when he would get angry.

"They're kids," said Char with an air of surprise.

I heard Nickie's breathing shudder and I knew she was about

to start crying. "Please," managed to pass through my lips.

"What are you doing in my house?" Mazie asked. The tone of her voice was stern as her eyes narrowed.

"We didn't know this was your house," I said. "Or anyone's house. We're sorry. We were just trying to get out of the rain."

"Please don't turn us in," Nickie said through her tears. She took a sharp breath. Her hand frantically hit my arm.

I turned to see her grasping at the collar of her shirt. Fear showed in her normally carefree blue eyes. Ignoring the women, I tried to get my fingers into the mock turtleneck. The bluish-black collar began to tighten further.

"Nickie! Hang on!" I screamed.

My fingers could not loosen the collar from around her neck. I felt something cold next to my finger.

"Don't move," Mazie said. "The shirt is trying to mend itself. Char, grab this side. You, pull away that side." Her hand glided a metal blade through the recycled plastic fibers of Nickie's shirt. The three of us cut the shirt down the middle. Char pulled the shirt off of Nickie from behind, while Mazie grabbed a blanket and threw it over Nickie's torso.

Under the blanket, Nickie rubbed her neck. "Thanks," she said with some difficulty. "I wonder if that was what has been attacking people, Xav," said Nickie quietly. "That's why Mom and Dad are gone. They knew."

Mazie and Char exchanged looks. Char left without saying a word. My first thought was that she left to call someone to collect us.

"Take that shirt off, too," Maize instructed me. "I won't have anyone dying in my house."

Pulling the still wet shirt over my head, the stale air gave my skin goosebumps. I was envious of Nickie's blanket.

When Char returned, she threw a pile of material on the couch. "Find something that fits, kids," she said.

Nickie found a shirt quickly, but I hesitated to rummage through the pile. "Are you turning us in?" I asked.

"To whom?" said Mazie.

"PC one-five," Nickie answered.

Char made a sound of disapproval. "We like being free, despite the lack of modernity," she said.

Finally, I pulled a gray blob over my head that instantly warmed me. When my head emerged from the collar, Char was gone. Mazie picked the lighted jar off the table. Her hard lined face softened some.

"You kids need some warming," she said. "Come on."

We followed her through a doorway into a hallway with peeling walls. In the limited light, the house revealed its years of neglect. In another room, more lighted jars greeted us. Sitting at a table with Mazie, the room appeared to be a kitchen. Char leaned against the cabinets next to a stove with a blue light under a pot.

"Ma'am," Nickie said.

"Please, call me Mazie."

Nickie smiled. "Mazie," she said, "what are these jar lights?"

Mazie's eyebrows raised. "Homemade oil lamps," she explained.

Char set mugs in front of Nickie and me. When Char poured hot tea into the mugs, Mazie continued, "Drink some tea to get warm. I'll be back soon." She walked away. Char sat with us, grasping a mug of her own.

Taking a sip, I cherished the warm drink. The mug warmed my hands nicely as the tea warmed my core.

Nickie tapped the mug with her fingernail. The sound it made was not the dull thunk we were used to hearing from our hard plastic mugs at home. "What's this made from?" Nickie asked Char.

"Teabags and hot water," Char answered, looking puzzled.

"No, I meant the mug."

"It's stoneware," Char said. She looked at each of us. "As you probably know by now I'm Char. You are Nickie and?" she looked at me.

Her very short, spiky, blonde hair cast strange shadows in the lamplight. "Xavier," I answered.

She smiled at me, exposing laugh lines on the outside of her brown eyes. "Not many escape the Pod Cities," she said. "You two are lucky, especially given your age."

"Bring them upstairs," Mazie called, "with light."

Finishing our tea, Nickie and I followed Char down the hallway with the peeling walls. We climbed rickety stairs that creaked with each step. The light from our oil lamps revealed more peeling walls with faded colors.

Mazie met us at the top of the stairs. "Change into some clean, dry clothes," she said. "You should be able to find something that fits. My grandmother kept everything." She pointed us towards different rooms. "Change your shoes and socks, too, if you can."

Entering a bedroom, I placed the lamp on a extremely dusty dresser. Through the thick dust, the room looked as though it was a boy's room at one time. Opening drawers, I rummaged to find a pair of thick blue pants, socks and a t-shirt. I threw everything on the large, dusty bed. As I removed my clothes, I finally realized how wet I had become. The dry clothes felt great against my body. I opened the closet door and found shoes that fit. At least, in premise.

I heard a gentle knock on the door. "Xavier," said Mazie's voice, "may I come in?"

"Yeah."

Opening the door, she looked at my feet. With a soft smile on her face, she said, "Your sister needed some help with those, too." She crouched down and tugged on the shoes. "Let me guess, you've never tied shoelaces."

Never thinking of shoelaces, I shook my head. There I was, wondering where the zippers were. As I watched her tie the laces, I missed my parents immensely.

"How do they feel?" she asked as she looked at me curiously.

Wiggling my feet a little, I answered, "Good."

As she stood, she said, "Give Char your old clothes. She'll take care of them for you."

Gathering my clothes, I handed them to Char who was waiting in the hallway.

Nickie greeted me at the top of the stairs, wearing pants and shoes similar to mine. We followed Mazie down the creaky stairs.

All the oil lamps but one were returned to the kitchen and extinguished. Char walked into the kitchen. She gave Mazie a nod, then blew out her lamp.

"Time to go," Mazie said.

We followed Mazie in the dim light to an opened door. I figured it was the same door they came through. Mazie stepped down. Her feet made hollow thumping sounds with each step. As we followed, the thuds from our feet reverberated off all the hard surfaces. Mazie's oil lamp illuminated painted stone walls. In the lamplight, I saw Nickie's nose wrinkle from the damp smell.

We walked behind a stack of junk that hid a dark hole in the floor. "Watch your step," said Mazie. She disappeared into the hole. I was not entirely sure about climbing into a dark, smelly hole under an old house that could have possibly fallen down around us at any moment with strange women we barely knew. Yet, it was a better option then facing the repercussions from running away.

That was what we did after all—run away. Away from our pain, from our sorrow, and from whatever life held for us back in PC one-five. We ran, knowing that we could never return. But, we had nothing for which to return. A group home and mandatory Protector Unit duty was hardly worth it. The unknown of the wilderness was better than the unknown of the so-called civilization.

At the bottom of the dark stairs, Mazie's oil lamp shone bright concrete walls, ceiling and floor. We walked down a long, concrete tunnel that echoed each breath. Every so often, we passed bulges along the walls that were reminiscent of lights. Silently, I wondered what happened to the electricity.

After walking for some time, the bulges flickered a few times.

"Brayden's trying to get it working again," Char mentioned. "I don't think that man ever sleeps."

"Get what working?" Nickie asked.

"Generator," Mazie explained. "One they can't detect," she added darkly.

"I don't understand," said Nickie.

Char walked next to her. "These tunnels were built as part of a larger bomb shelter complex, before they shut down the electrical grids."

"Why did they do that?"

"Security reasons," Char said as her fingers made air quotes.

"They haven't been turned back on?" I asked.

"Can't," Mazie said as she stopped next to a large, metal wheel on the wall. Turning the wheel, she continued, "The grids were hit with electromagnetic pulses. Nothing worked right afterwards."

When she could no longer turn the wheel, an oval door opened. Air sounded like it was being released. Stepping over the threshold, we entered a cavernous, cement room with many oval metal doors. Against the walls, were multiple wheels, at least one for each door. Both Char and Mazie each turned a wheel. Char's wheel closed the door through which we came. Mazie's wheel opened a new door.

"Sleep down here for what night remains," Mazie said. She beckoned us across the room. Her oil lamp illuminated a room full of bunk beds at least four high. "Breakfast will be topside. One of us will wake you when it's morning."

We picked beds near the open door. "Thank you," said Nickie. I thought I caught a rare glimpse of a smile on Mazie's face before she left us in the dark.

Chapter 5

"Time to get up," Char's cheery voice said way too early. I felt as though we had just fallen asleep.

"Is it morning already?" Nickie asked. She rubbed her face with her one hand.

Char pressed a wet cloth and a toothbrush into our hands. "For washing," she explained. "You're gonna wanna eat. I'll wait for you out here." Giving us a wide smile, she stepped over the high threshold.

After washing my face and brushing my teeth, I walked over to my sister. Her eyelids drooped a little. "Where do you think she's taking us?" I whispered.

She rolled her eyes. "Oh, *now* you're suspicious," she whispered back. "I have a good feeling about them." Sliding off her bed, she added, "They didn't let me choke to death." Nickie placed her wet rag and used toothbrush in my hand, then left me alone in the dark room.

Walking out of the room, I gave the rags and brushes to a waiting Char. While I waited for her to turn wheels, I realized that it was Nickie's feelings that got us standing in an underground bunker. Another oval door opened revealing round, metal rungs of a ladder against the wall of a tiny hole of a room.

Ushering us into the hole, Char squeezed in, closing the door behind us. She pushed past us, saying, "Come on up."

I allowed Nickie to grab the rungs before me. As we climbed, Char babbled.

"Mazie already told the mayor about you two," Char said. "You are going to have to meet him this morning. Nothing to be scared of, by the way. We live in a small community. All newcomers should see the mayor. That way, we know who's here. Stop climbing. Need to open the hatch."

I heard Char turning yet another wheel. After a soft plunging noise, we emerged from the hole. I looked around a small, dark room while Char closed the hatch. The room smelled of old dirt. When Char opened a door, sunlight bathed the tiny room. As my eyes adjusted to the brightness, I could see shining metal objects hanging from hooks on the wall. The hole from which we came blended with the other gray squares on the floor. On the other side of the opened door stood Mazie.

"Breakfast first," said Mazie.

As we followed her through the long grass, I became mesmerized with multiple gray strands of hair reflecting the morning sunlight. The grass ended at a broken cement sidewalk. Roots from old trees poked through the cracks, giving the sidewalk more hills and dales than it should have had.

Old buildings surrounded us. Some of them met the old broken sidewalk; some were a bit further back. Most had broken windows and gaping holes in their roofs and walls, which gave me the creeps.

After looking around, Nickie asked, "What happened here?"

Any of Mazie's warmness melted off her face. "You're walking through the remnants of a town abandoned," she explained.

"Oh," said Nickie. "After the plague."

"What plague?" asked Char.

Nickie and I exchanged looks. For our entire lives, we had been told about the plague that decimated the population of the United States because our ancestors did not care enough about the planet. The survivors were forced to burn down the dirty, disease-infested cities and rebuild cleaner, more ecologically sustainable communities. Before the cleansing, the air was so thick with pollution it was hard to breathe without using a respirator. A lot of replanting took place to make the air breathable. Organic farming practices and recycling programs saved us from the brink of extinction. Wild animals were reintroduced to their natural habitats to help restore the natural balance of the ecosystems. The old cities were replaced with clusters of green pods made entirely from recycled materials.

In these Pod Cities, survivors and their descendants started anew to live and work in harmony with the environment. Emission free electric pod cars took people around the city on zero polluting rails. Electrified fences surrounded each Pod City in an effort to keep urban sprawl from returning so that people could not impose upon the environment. High-speed magnetic trains connected each Pod City across the country with minimal environmental impact. I wondered how Char did not know.

"Pod City," muttered Mazie.

"Right," Char said.

The broken sidewalk brought us to an open area with lots of long tables with benches underneath a roof. People of all ages sat with bowls, talking happily to one another. Mazie led us to an empty area.

"Sit here," she said. "We'll be right back with breakfast."

Nickie and I sat across from each other at the wooden table. While my eyes followed Mazie and Char to a couple of people who stood near a large black pot, Nickie's eyes examined the covered area.

"Look at all the people," Nickie said quietly. "I didn't expect there to be so many people."

I looked around. People filled almost every table. When we set off into the wilderness, I was not sure what to expect. In school, they told us that only we survived—the ones who lived in the pod cities. Obviously, *they* were wrong.

Mazie and Char arrived, carrying two bowls each. One was placed in front of me. I stared at the steaming tan and beige speckled lumps in the bowl. "What is it?" I asked.

"Oatmeal," Char answered as she poured a little thick, dark amber liquid into her bowl.

I stared at the contents of my bowl again. It was not any oatmeal with which I was familiar. Oatmeal was all boring beige and mushy straight from the microwave.

"Maple syrup?" offered Char. She placed a pitcher on the

table in front of Nickie and me.

We looked at the pitcher then at each other. "Maple syrup is illegal," said Nickie.

"Not here," Char said before happily spooning oatmeal into her mouth.

"Let me guess," said Mazie. "Those poor sugar maple trees. How dare we awful, awful humans steal their sap? It's akin to raping the trees for our own selfish means."

Nickie nodded her head.

Rolling her eyes, Mazie said, "It is a less refined product than corn syrup and actually has some nutrients. Try it. If you don't like it, you don't have to eat it."

I allowed Nickie to go first. Picking up the pitcher, she poured a little onto her spoon. She sniffed it, very unsure. Tasting it, she said, "It's good. Different, but good."

When she was done, I did not bother to examine it. Pouring it on, I just ate. It was definitely a hardier flavor than what I was used to eating, but I did not care. Food was food. What surprised me was Nickie's reluctance to use the maple syrup. Sure, it was illegal, but so was ditching our jackets, then running away from PC one-five.

Finishing our breakfast, Mazie said, "Come on, kids. Time to see the mayor."

Char took our bowls while Mazie led us out of the covered eating area. We walked along broken concrete under overgrown trees. Once we left the cover of the trees, we saw a yellow brick building.

The broken concrete continued to a broken glass door that was crudely patched with rusted red metal. When Mazie opened the door, we walked into a dark hallway. Sunlight tried to reach through opened doors onto the dingy carpet. Glancing through one of the open doorways, I saw a man sitting at a desk, completely engrossed with his papers. The desk was devoid of electrical devices. Through another open doorway, a woman used a long stick thing on a piece of paper.

At the end of the hall was a set of metal doors. Beside the doors, Mazie began to climb metal stairs. We followed her up three flights of stairs. The stairs ended at a gray metal door. She opened the door, ushering us into another hallway. We walked past more opened doors until we reached a woman sitting at a desk.

The woman's blonde hair was hastily pinned on the top of her head. Looking up at us, she said, "Good morning, Mazie."

"Morning, Beryl," Mazie said. "I have an appointment with Jotham."

Beryl looked at a book on her desk. "Yes, you do. Follow me."

She took us behind a wooden partition. We followed her past a u-shaped seating configuration to a wood and glass door. I could barely make out the word *mayor* in the faded black block lettering on the glass. Beryl knocked on the door, then opened it without waiting for a response.

"Your first appointment is here," Beryl said as she stood to the side, allowing us to enter the small room.

"Thank you, Beryl," said a cheery, rather deep, voice.

From behind Mazie, I saw a tall man with a long graying beard and matching mustache rise out of a dark chair behind a desk. Walking around the desk, he greeted Mazie.

"Mazie, how nice it is to see you again so soon," he said while shaking her hand. "Are these the children?"

"Indeed," said Mazie. She did not seem to be as thrilled to see him as he was to see her. "Kids, this is Jotham, the mayor of our little community. Jotham, Xavier and Nickie."

His dark eyes looked at each of us while the sunlight shone through the thinning gray hair on the top of his head. "Sit down, please," he said. As we sat, Jotham continued, "Escapees from Pod City one-five. How very exciting. You must tell me how you achieved it." He smiled widely.

Jotham looked friendly enough, but there was something about him of which I was not sure. Nickie did not seem to want to open her mouth, so I had to speak.

"We just buried our mother," I began.

"I'm so sorry," said Jotham.

"Thank you," I said. "Just after burying our father." Their gravestone was so clear in my memory.

"Orphans? How tragic," he said too animated for my taste.

I nodded my head, then continued. "A tree in their memory was planted. So, we were given permission to visit it."

"After we spent some time at the tree," Nickie said with tears in her eyes, "we were returning to the picnic area. There was a small black bear rummaging through our food."

I sat there, trying not to look as if it was the first time I had heard the story.

"And of course where there is a small bear, a big bear is not far behind," she said. "I guess it thought we were threatening its cub. Our first instinct was to run. Well, it chased us and chased us. Eventually, it left us alone. We were in the middle of unfamiliar woods, but we dared not return—afraid that it was still eating our food. So, we decided to wait it out. That's when it began to rain. The storm made everything dark. I was so scared." Nickie paused to wipe tears from her eyes. "Completely lost, we kept walking in all sorts of directions. Eventually, we found Mazie."

"And the rest, as they say, is history," said Jotham with a smile.

Chapter 6

Nickie covered her face with her hands. Her whole body bounced as she cried uncontrollably.

"I know it's difficult," said Mazie with her hand stroking Nickie's back, "but, it will be all right."

"Ah. Well," uttered Jotham who looked upon Nickie as some discarded, deformed creature. "Go see, what's-her-face in the library. She'll get you situated and whatnot." Jumping off his chair, he quickly made his way to the door. Opening it, he said, "Well, you seem like good kids. Glad you survived. See you around."

A smile plastered on Jotham's face as we walked out of his office. Nickie's tears dried by the time we were walking down the stairs. Outside the yellow brick building, we crossed an expanse of a neglected black parking lot. We arrived at a small, beige brick building with the metal letters, *ubl c L br y*, rusting against the brick.

The glass doors clearly used to open electronically. Walking inside, rows upon rows of books behind a circular wooden desk greeted us. A sign on the desk said, "Ring bell for service." Mazie tapped the top of a shiny dome next to the sign.

Not long after the ding reverberated in my ears, a woman older than I have ever met before lifted a panel of the desktop. Standing in the center, she said with a smile, "How can I help you today?"

"I have two new residents," said Mazie, returning the woman's smile.

"Then we need some forms," the woman said. After digging in a drawer, she placed two pieces of paper on top of the desk. "Just a few quick questions, then I'll put you in the register." Smiling, she opened a small glass bottle, then grabbed a pen.

"We will start with you, young lady," she said. Dipping the point of the pen into the bottle, she began. "Spell your full name for me, please."

"N-I-C-O-L-E," said Nickie. "K-E-L-T-O-N."

"Thank you." She smiled. "Obviously female. Date of birth?"

"Day thirty-seven, year six," Nickie answered.

The woman's pen hovered over the paper. "I am going to leave the month and day blank and just put down the year." Her cheerful tone did not falter. "Let's see. That would be 2061." She moved onto the next piece of paper. Looking at me, she said, "Spell your name please."

"X-A-V-I-E-R," I answered. "K-E-L-T-O-N."

"Okay," she said. "And your date of birth?"

"Day one-hundred eighty-four, year three."

"Three," she repeated. "That would be 2058." Placing those papers to the side, she looked at us, saying, "Husband and wife or brother and sister."

"Siblings," answered Mazie. "They'll be residing with me."

"Of course," she said. "Can I help you with anything else today?"

Mazie said, "Yes. They need books on handwriting and history."

"Let me put these away first." Still smiling, she disappeared behind the desk for a moment. When she popped back up, she said, "Follow me."

Mazie stayed at the desk while we followed the woman through aisles of books that were squeezed onto shelves.

"You are allowed four books at a time," she told us. "When you bring them back, you can get more."

Nickie's eyes opened with awe as she glanced at the spines. While we walked throughout the library, the woman pulled books off the shelves. Arms full of books, we met Mazie at the counter. After the woman checked us out, we continued walking through the "abandoned" town.

From the broken sidewalk, I saw people walking in and out of buildings. I wondered what they were doing. We turned down other streets that took us to the edge of town.

Mazie took us to a small house at the end of the street. Opening a screen door, she said, "It isn't much, but it's home."

The front door opened into a sitting area with two small couches and a chair. The room was cozy and felt like a home.

"You can put your books on the coffee table," said Char, coming in from another room.

Nickie carefully placed her pile of books on the small wooden table. I put my books next to hers.

"Sit down," Mazie said.

Nickie and I sat next to each other on one of the couches. Mazie sat as close as possible to us on the other couch while Char pulled over the chair.

"Are we in trouble?" Nickie asked.

"Who are you?" asked Mazie in return.

Her face was so stern I thought it would crack. I could not get myself to say anything. Nickie opened her mouth, but Mazie threw two pieces of paper on the table. She took the forms from the library.

"The tears and the bear story were fake," said Mazie. "Explain yourselves."

When neither one of us were quick to respond, Mazie continued, "Who sent you here?"

"No one," I said. "We are who—"

"Our parents," interjected Nickie.

"That's what you believe, Nickie," I said.

"When Dad talked to us that last time," her eyes started to fill with wetness.

I could not argue with her.

"It's what he wanted. After he…, it's what they both wanted." Nickie succumbed to her tears.

Mazie looked from her to me. "Let's start with who your parents are."

"Caleb and Sadie Kelton," I said.

Mazie leaned back a little. I told her and Char how they worked for the different commissions. When I explained what we were told about the white farmhouse, a tear streaked down Mazie's cheek.

After talking about the funerals, Mazie said, "No bodies to bury? Are you sure they are dead?"

"Yes," I said.

"No," said Nickie.

"How did you escape?" Mazie asked softly.

I remembered it all too well. My mind played the picture while Nickie told Mazie and Char the story.

We stood listening to the river like always, but without Mom and Dad. Dark clouds blew in from the other side of the river. Nickie slid her jacket down her arms, setting it on the ground. She looked at me and without saying a word, asked me why I was not doing the same. It was Dad's idea, after all, to offer our jackets to the river. Not thinking about what would come next, I slid my jacket off, then placed it on top of Nickie's.

The wind whipped through our hair. Nickie took a deep breath. Picking up the jackets, she walked closer to the rushing water. With great force, she hurled our jackets into the air. She slipped a little, but I caught her.

I watched the dark jackets flap against the graying sky. They landed gracefully on top of the water. Within seconds, the river took them under.

Sparks emitted from the water with cracking noises. We took a few steps backwards. A low wail reached our ears. Fear flashed across Nickie's face. Grabbing hands, we climbed up the riverbank, then ran.

Chapter 7

When Nickie stopped talking, Mazie looked at us for a few seconds. Reaching for the papers with our names on them, she thrust them at Char. "To burn," she said.

"Why?" Nickie asked.

"And stick with the bear story," Mazie added.

"No paper trail," answered Char who took the papers, then left the room.

Nickie watched Char leave. "I don't understand," she said to Mazie.

"Just in case," Mazie said. She smiled warmly. "Now, Nickie, you will attend school. Xavier, since you're over sixteen, we have to find you a job."

"What do you and Char do?" Nickie asked.

"In a former life, I used to be an architect," Mazie said. "Here, I'm the building inspector."

"I was a general contractor," said Char, entering the room. "I fix things and help Brayden with the defunct generator. What's your forte?" She returned to her chair.

"I," I had a hard time answering. The job chose you rather you choosing the job in PC one-five.

Rolling her eyes, Nickie answered for me. "He's great with electrical devices."

"Then, it's generator work for you," said Char. "I'll introduce you to Brayden today."

"And I'll take Nickie to see Exie," Mazie said. "She's the head of the school," she added.

"Meet at the Pavilion for lunch," said Char. "Come on, kid, this is going to be fun." She wore a wide smile as she leapt from her seat.

Leaving Nickie with Mazie, I followed Char into a small hall. After opening a door, she said, "After you."

I walked down carpeted stairs. The only light shone through the opened door. Char closed the door behind us, plunging us into darkness. I heard a scrape, then saw light. Continuing down the steps, I came to a landing where I waited for Char.

"I know it's dark," she said, "but such is the nature of basements." She whizzed by me.

I followed her down the last couple of steps into a cozy sitting area. Placing the lamp on the table, she picked up a long thin stick. Char placed the tip into the flame until the stick caught fire.

Blowing out the lamp, she said, "Stay close."

We walked past the old couches and through an opened door. The small flame barely illuminated a cramped bedroom. Amongst the bed, dresser, tall chest, and two massive wardrobes, Char made a beeline for a narrow, three-drawer chest covered with chotchkies.

Standing in front, she touched over half of them in what I thought was a deliberate order. I heard the soft unplugging of a drain. The small chest glided forward, taking part of the carpet with it.

With one hand, Char lifted a square piece of wood that had been slightly raised at one end. She lowered her flame into a person-sized hole under the wood for a few seconds, then said, "Take a lantern from the wall on your way down."

As I climbed into the hole, I saw a metal encasement hanging from a nail. The light only shone towards the wall. I grabbed it by its wire handle and climbed down the ladder. Char climbed onto the rungs above me after taking her own lantern.

Journeying down the hole was relatively short. The ladder ended at a long, dark corridor. When Char joined me, she walked to the other side. Her lantern illuminated a bunch of wheeled contraptions.

"Pick a bike. Except this gray one. That one's mine," she told me.

I froze. I had read about bicycles, but I had never ridden one.

"What's wrong?" Char asked. Facing her lantern towards me, she said, "Oh. Don't know how to ride. It's easy. Here, take this one." She wheeled a blue one towards me. "Hang your lantern on the hook on the front."

I did as she said, barely noticing how the corridor had been lit.

Standing side by side with our bikes, she said, "Riding a bike is the easiest thing ever. Peddling makes you go. Handlebars steer. Left hand is for your back brake. Right hand is for your front brake. Once you stop, put your foot down. Balance comes naturally."

She gave me a smile, then swung her leg over the bike. I followed her example putting my right foot on the pedal. With a deep breath, I pushed. My left foot found the other pedal. My legs moved in a strange circular motion while my arms were trying to keep the bike straight instead of side to side. Eventually, my hunch straightened and I was able to be excited about riding a bike for the first time.

"See, I told you it was easy," Char said. "You're doing well."

My whole body joined in exhilaration. Even though I was riding in a tunnel somewhere underground, I felt free. Oval metal doors and wheels dotted the otherwise smooth walls of the long, gray corridor. Char stayed a half of bike length ahead of me.

"Our door is coming up," announced Char. "Start slowing down."

Taking my eyes off of the tunnel for a moment, I glanced down at the handlebars. The brake levers shone in the dim light. "Which one?" I yelled in a panic.

As I passed Char, she said, "Right hand."

Without taking my palm off the handlebar, my fingers reached for the shiny lever. The metal was cold under my fingertips. Not wanting to go too far from Char, I squeezed the lever.

My momentum abruptly stopped. I could feel the back wheel lift off the ground. Leaning backwards, the bike and I began to tip sideways.

"Feet on the ground!"

I heard Char, but my feet did not want to separate from the pedals. In slow motion, the tunnel went from vertical to horizontal. A dull clang rang in my ears as I laid on the floor with the bike in-between my legs.

"You all right?" Char asked. She stood over me with a lantern in her hand.

"Yeah," I said while trying to untangle myself from the blue bike.

Char helped me to my feet. After I lifted the bike off the floor, Char said, "Lean the bike against the wall next to mine. Here's your lantern."

Hanging the lantern back on the bike, I walked it to where Char's bike waited. As I steadied the bike against the wall, I heard a door open.

Returning to her bike, Char said, "Grab your lantern. Follow me."

Lantern in hand, I stepped over the threshold. Char closed the door behind us, then we walked through another tunnel.

"This is a direct tunnel to the generator. It's the only one, too. Anywhere else takes you to the prep room," explained Char. "Brayden is an older gentleman. Now, he tells everyone that he used to be an electrician. Though I think he was more of an electrical engineer or something like that. I should warn you that he's, uh, how should I put it, protective, suspicious and cynical."

We reached the end of the tunnel. Turning the wheel, Char continued, "A lot of people got like that after the war—distrusting I mean."

"What war?" I asked.

"*The* war," said Char. The door opened, then Char said, "Generator time."

Chapter 8

When I walked through the oval opening, my jaw dropped. In the middle of the round room was a multilevel metal monstrosity. A soft whirring hum reached my ears. Dim electric lights were perched along the walls. Spotlight lamps adorned the rails, separating the walkway from the generator. Despite the presence of electricity, we still needed our lanterns to see properly.

I followed Char around the generator. A third of the way around, a man's legs stuck out from underneath a massive metal contraption with all sorts of buttons, screens and gauges.

"This is the generator's control panel," Char explained.

"'Bout time you showed up, Char," said the man's raspy voice from underneath the control panel. "There's a short."

"Another one?" Char said.

"Only I don't know where it is," he said as his head emerged. He looked at me with his beady eyes. "Who are you?" he asked.

Transfixed on his scruffy short beard, I did not answer.

"Brayden," said Char, "this is Xavier."

"I'm sick of that school sending me their graduate flunkies to apprentice with me," Brayden complained while wiping his short forehead just above his very bushy eyebrows with a dirty looking cloth.

"He's not going anywhere," Char said with her hands on her hips.

Brayden ran a stubby thumb down the side of his unshaved jaw line. "Fine," he said. "But, I'm not teaching him." Placing the rag onto the edge of a toolbox, he continued, "Char, I need you on the lower level, section four-nine b. You," he pointed to me, "stay here. Touch nothing."

Their footsteps clanged as they descended the metal steps along the wall. I did not quite know what I was supposed to do there if Brayden did not want me touching anything. Putting my hands behind my back, I gazed at the control panel. The technology was ancient—actual keyboards instead of touchpads. The more I looked, the more I realized how familiar it was. It was reminiscent of my scrollpad just on a bigger scale.

Glancing over the railing, I saw the shadows of Brayden and Char on the other side of the generator. I crouched down to try to see under the control panel. Not being able to see, I knelt, positioning my lantern to shine on the wiring. Somehow, I ended up on my back under the controls.

The wires were old and some of the circuitry had been scorched at one time. I knew he told me not to touch anything, but I just needed to try something. Before I knew it, I had begun making new connections.

"What are you doing?" scolded Brayden. "Get out from under there!"

"Two seconds," I said.

"Don't make me drag you."

Finishing my connection, I slid out from underneath the control panel.

"I told you not to touch," said Brayden, seething. "Don't they teach you to follow instructions at that school? What about your parents? Didn't they teach you anything?"

Before standing, my finger just happened to press the power switch. When the monitors flickered on, Brayden quieted.

"Told you so," Char said to Brayden.

Approaching the control panel, Brayden eyed me suspiciously. He tapped quickly on the keyboard before turning to face me. "What did you do?" he asked me.

"Bypassed the short," I answered. "Too much current ran through the wires. The regulator couldn't handle all that current. The way I reconnected everything, there will be no more problems with the amount of electrical current."

He took a step towards me, pinning me against the metal railing. A sharp blade grazed my neck.

"Brayden!" said Char. "Are you mad?"

Ignoring Char, he said, "Where did you learn all that?" His raspy voice was steady and direct. "*Who* taught you?"

My back bent over the rail in an attempt to keep away from his blade. "I did," I managed to say.

"Where?" he asked. His face inched closer to mine.

"Put the knife away!" yelled Char.

"PC—" I began.

"A Pod City?" said Brayden, his eyes narrowing. "Did they send you to spy on us? Sabotage our attempts for electricity even further?"

"He's not a plant," Char pleaded.

"The young ones don't attempt to leave the Pod Cities," Brayden said with his eyes boring into mine. "They'd be too brainwashed and have no memory of what was. Sorry, Char, he may have charmed you, but he's not going to pull a fast one on me. You planting tracking devices, so they can eradicate us all? Is their new policy, if they can't control us, kill us?"

"*They* killed his parents," exasperated Char. "Now, put down the knife."

"Tell me," he said through gritted teeth.

The blade of the knife still grazed my skin while I said, "My dad discovered a series of lies and cover-ups. After he discussed it with my mom, they were both dead within weeks." Those words flowed from my mouth like I was purging a poison.

Brayden lowered his knife, then took a step backwards. Although my body straightened, I did not dare move away from the railing.

"They killed my people, too," said Brayden in a low voice. Turning away from me, he checked the screens. "Char, get me paper from the office," he barked. "We have a horde of problems."

Char put a comforting hand on my arm before disappearing through a door. Whatever comfort I felt left with her. I stood attached to the railing, afraid to move anywhere in the expansive, dim room.

It felt as though years had passed before Char returned. She smiled at me while we waited for Brayden to finish scribbling on the paper.

"Let's get it fixed," said Brayden with sheets of paper in his hand. He stashed a pencil behind his ear, then grabbed his toolbox. I watched Char follow him to the steps. When he got to the first step, he looked back, saying, "Are you coming, Kid?"

Disconnecting myself from the railing, I ran to catch up with them. From the bottom of the steps, we walked around the humming generator. The dim lights flickered as Brayden grabbed tools from his box.

After he removed an access panel, Brayden said, "Do your thing, Kid. Then we'll fix the parts that need fixing."

I stepped in front of the two feet by three feet section. Looking at the mishmash of wires, my palms got sweaty and my heart raced. No one had ever watched me work. I wiped my hands on my shirt before touching the wires. With a deep breath, I pretended that I was alone, in my room of my family's condo, tweaking my scrollpad. As I disconnected wires, the solitary confines of my memories disappeared when Brayden walked away. Without his beady eyes boring into the back of my neck, I found that I did not need my imagined world. When I finished, three damaged circuit boards were bypassed.

"Done? Good," said Brayden. "You can get started on the next section, while Char and I finish up here."

The next section happened to be two floors above where Char and Brayden were working. Part of me relished in being alone for the first time in a long time. Part of me could not fathom how many circuits were bad. Part of me wondered how Nickie's day was going. Part of me missed Mom and Dad terribly. Then, another part of me wished that I were not working alone.

After a couple of hours, a voice interrupted my work.

"How goes it?" Brayden asked.

"Slow," I said, making connections. "This section is really damaged."

"Thought it would be," said Brayden. "Closer to all the outside connections."

Poking my head out of the mess of wires, I managed to look at Brayden. "How did this happen?" I asked.

"Combination of not enough failsafes and lack of sufficient ground," answered Brayden. "Whoever put this place together, in their infinite wisdom," he rolled his eyes, "connected the generator to outside sources of electricity. When the electromagnetic pulse hit, it traveled down the wires to the generator. I can't tell you how much I have replaced on this rust bucket since I arrived here. At least I was able to get it from not working to barely working."

"You keep talking his ear off, Brayden, we're going to miss lunch," Char said.

"Lunch?" he asked as if it were a foreign concept.

"Promised Mazie," said Char. "Come on, Xavier, you can finish when we get back."

Hungry, I followed Char through a different door whose ladder brought us to an abandoned building, or so I thought. We walked out of a room with covered windows and chipped paint into a narrow hallway. At the end of the hall, old men sat on chairs around a small table. They held small colored papers.

One glanced at us. "How's the card game going boys?" Char asked.

"Eh," the one who looked at us said. "I've had better luck but, I can't complain too much."

"The trick to playing a good hand of poker is to watch the bluff and don't get beaten by the royal flush," said another.

With a small nod, Char led me out the front door. Once we were walking down the street, I asked, "What was that about?"

"They're security guards," Char said.

"In a beat up old house?" It made no sense to me.

"Gotta protect what you have," said Char as we approached the pavilion, "even if you don't have much."

Chapter 9

Under the shade of the roof, I spotted Nickie sitting with a group of teenagers. Nickie waved me over. As I crossed the pavilion, I noticed Char and Mazie swapping stories.

"Xav," Nickie said, "I want you to meet some people." She gestured across from her, saying, "This is Jett."

My eyes followed her hand. I gave a weak smile to the dark haired boy who looked to be around my age.

"Sorrel," continued Nickie.

He nodded his blond head at me in greeting.

"Jennara."

I caught Jennara staring at me. Her bright hair sparkled when she smiled.

"And Kai," Nickie finished.

My eyes locked with deep blue orbs. Her long dark hair framed her face in beautiful cascading waves.

"Join us," said Jett.

Breaking my gaze, I sat at the table.

"You need food," Nickie said. She jumped off the bench leaving me with her new friends.

"Out of school must be great," Jett said to me. "I'm taking my finals in a few weeks."

"You think Whitetail will take you on as his apprentice?" asked Sorrel.

"I hope so," Jett said.

Nickie returned with my lunch. Taking a bite of my sandwich, I listened to the conversation.

"Hopefully, he won't just let you linger in the woods for days like he's done to others," said Jennara, smirking. "He hasn't taken on an apprentice in ages. What makes you think he'll take you?"

"Because I'm not afraid of him," Jett quipped.

Washing down my lunch with drink, I asked, "Who is Whitetail?"

"Only the best survivalist ever," said Sorrel, obviously enamored.

"Basically, you don't find him," said Kai. "*He* finds you."

Sorrel looked over his shoulder. "Time to go guys," he said. "Nice meeting you, Xavier."

Getting up, they all said, "Bye," to me. I swear I saw Kai smile at me, but I might have been seeing things—wishful thinking. Nickie waved as she left me sitting at the table by myself to finish my lunch.

I stared out into nowhere, chewing mindlessly. Finding the conversation about Whitetail intriguing, my mind replayed Kai's words, *he finds you*. The words alone sounded sinister. However, they all seemed to have been in awe of the illusive man. While I pondered, Char plopped on the bench next to me.

"About ready?" Char asked.

Drinking the last of my juice, I said, "Yup."

While we walked through the town, I asked, "Char, who is Whitetail?"

"A myth," she told me.

"How does someone apprentice with a myth?"

She chuckled. "They want to believe."

Entering the house, Char gave the men a friendly nod. As we continued down the hall, she said, "People will wander into the mountains, searching for him. After a few days, they return believing that they weren't worthy of him." She kept talking while we climbed down the hatch. "Some people have been severely injured trying to find him." At the bottom of the ladder, Char looked straight at me. "Those who didn't return were believed to have been taken on as an apprentice until the next person who treks up there finds a mauled body."

Every muscle in my body tightened. It must have shown because Char was quick to answer.

"We have to remind ourselves," she said, "that the powers that be are not the only dangers out there."

For the remainder of the afternoon, Brayden kept me so busy that I had no time to think about Whitetail or anything for that matter. I was working alone in an obscure section of the generator when Brayden nonchalantly strolled behind me. After passing me a few times, he stopped. When I stepped away from the generator, he opened his mouth.

"I, uh," he said. "You do good work."

"Thanks."

"About earlier, with the knife," Brayden said with his hands deep in his pockets. "Sorry about that."

Opening my mouth to speak, he stopped me.

"I owe you an explanation," he said. "When I was your age, I joined the Navy. That's when I learned my trade. I was a Naval Mechanic. Trained on both aircraft carriers and nuclear submarines. When the war started, we in the military were asked to do dastardly things." Pausing, he closed his eyes. "As much as I don't want to remember, forgetting would be worse. I'll spare you the details. My ship was in port during the transition. They came aboard and slaughtered whomever they considered dissidents. A bunch of us boarded inflatable life rafts. Jumped ship in the dead of night. My raft floated upriver. Every so often, one person would disembark. Each one of us went our separate ways. I haven't seen any of them for about twenty-five years. Settled here about twelve years ago. People don't ask much and that's just the way I like it." He moved his left foot as if he were going to leave, then stopped. "Keep all of it to yourself, mind you," said Brayden before leaving me to finish for the evening.

The return bike ride did not add any more bruises. Although I remembered to put my feet down, I still hit the wall with the tire.

Char chuckled. As we climbed into the house, she blabbered about growing up with her twin sister.

Ascending out of the basement, we heard a man's voice. Turning towards me, she pressed a finger to her lips. Char opened the door slowly. We tiptoed into the kitchen to eavesdrop.

"You can't protect that boy, Mazie," said the man's voice.

"Leave, Jotham," Mazie said in a cold voice. "Don't make me tell you again. I can't believe you would sell us out like that."

"It's for the good of the community," said Jotham.

"By community, you mean you," Mazie retorted. "Exie'd filet you."

"It doesn't have to be like that, Mazie," cooed Jotham.

"Get away from me," warned Mazie.

I heard a table fall.

"Get off me," Mazie pleaded. She sounded scared.

Opening a kitchen cabinet, Char snatched two guns. In the darkening kitchen, they looked just like standard Protector issue. Handing one to me, she breathed, "Point and squeeze if need be." I watched her disappear.

"No one will hear you scream," Jotham said softly.

I clutched the cold metal tightly.

"Mmm, I love me a fighter. Bite me again," Jotham taunted.

More furnishings sounded as if they were being knocked aside.

"Makes things that much more exciting. Don't you think?" Jotham said.

My stomach turned.

"I'll give you two seconds to get your hands off her," said Char.

"I'd ask you to join us, Char, but I know it's not your thing," said Jotham.

"No one will care when I shoot you dead, Jotham," Char said coldly. "Trust me."

A loud bang reverberated throughout the small house. Nickie came running into the kitchen. When she saw the gun in my hand, her eyes widened.

Char entered the kitchen then placed her gun on the counter. "He's gone," she said. "Only grazed his arm." She sounded disappointed. "Mazie is a bit shaken. Would one of you fill the kettle with water?"

I stood frozen with the gun still stuck to my hand. Nickie grabbed the kettle to fill it.

Char brought Mazie into the kitchen. She sat her in a chair. "You can put the gun down now," Char said before showing Nickie how to use the stove.

I placed the gun on the counter next to Char's. Sitting with Mazie, I asked, "Are you okay?"

She stared into the hallway. "That low... good-for-nothing... piece of... I'll kill him," said Mazie. Hardness set in her eyes. I could tell that she was planning and calculating.

When Char placed a steaming cup in front of Mazie, she snapped out of her scheming mode. "I'm fine, kids," she said. "Thanks for your concern. You can go back to reading, Nickie. And I'm sure you," looking at me, "want to get cleaned up after your hard day's work."

I did not feel grimy until Mazie suggested I shower. The water cleansed me of all I heard earlier, the guilt I felt from not believing Nickie, and the immense sorrow that I had been clutching so tightly. Climbing into pjs, I resolved to use that sorrow as a talisman.

After my shower, I knocked on Nickie's open door. She laid on the bed reading. Looking up from her book, she waved me inside.

I sat next to her on the bed. "So," I said.

Her eyebrows raised. "So?" she repeated.

I wanted to ask if we made the right decision, but I said, "How was school?"

"We're all in one room," she said. "And the teacher, Miss Exie, goes around to each of us. I'm learning how to write. I drew lines today!"

Her eyes sparkled. I knew my answer was yes.

"I'm also being taught *real* history. Did you know that three hundred years ago the American War for Independence began? They were fighting against an oppressive government. Miss Exie gave me this book to read. It's about the Revolutionary War and the Declaration of Independence. When I finish this, she is going to have me read the original Constitution. It is really interesting. Want me to see if she'll let you borrow it after I read it?"

Smiling at my sister's enthusiasm, I said, "Nah. Who will have time to read when the generator is a mess? You can give me the abridged version."

She laughed.

It was good to hear her laugh. Somehow, I joined her. Laughing made my whole body feel alive.

Exhausted, I crawled under the covers of my bed after visiting with Nickie. I fell asleep not too long after my head nestled in the pillow.

Mazie shook me awake in the darkness. "Hurry up; get dressed," she whispered.

"Mazie?" I said groggily. "What's going on?"

"Later," she said, looking out the window. "Get dressed. Quickly."

The urgency in her voice made me jump out of my warm bed. She ducked into the hall until I was attempting to tie my shoes. Mazie finished them for me.

"In here," she said, opening my closet door.

Completely confused, I followed Mazie into the closet. She closed the bi-fold doors behind us. Pushing aside the hanging clothes, she slid open a wall.

"Jump in," she instructed. "It's a slide."

I jumped down the dark hole. My bottom found a slick surface on which to rest. I, however, was not resting. Although I saw nothing, my other senses told me I was moving—fast.

The slide spit me out onto a padded surface. Standing, I saw two backpacks and what looked like a homemade flashlight at the floor of another chute.

Mazie gracefully exited the slide after me. Picking up the flashlight, she handed me a backpack. We secured them on our backs.

"Let's go," she said.

"What about Nickie?" I asked.

"Char will take care of her," she answered. "I showed her the chute. She's not in danger. *You* are."

"I don't understand," I said as we walked through an opening. Mazie's flashlight illuminated the dark tunnel wall.

She walked, counting under her breath. Stopping, she faced a cement section of wall. Mazie placed her right palm flat against the wall. A series of green lights flashed above Mazie's hand. I heard the familiar airlock release. In front of Mazie, a section of wall moved behind another.

We stepped into a roughly hewn tunnel. Mazie touched a series of numbers on a keypad, which closed the wall behind us.

When the keypad disappeared, Mazie said, "This way."

After a few steps, she explained, "Jotham came to visit while you and Char were working. He was going to turn you in to the Protector Units unless I gave him what he wanted."

"What did he want?"

She threw me a dark look. "My company," she said with disdain. "He's a creepy pig who thought he'd use you as leverage. Regardless of my answer, he would have turned you in anyway. He's been tipping off Protector Units about Pod City escapees' transfers from one settlement to another. In return for his trouble, he gets coal."

"Coal?" I said. I was confused. "I thought coal mining ended decades ago."

"That's what they want you to believe," said Mazie. "Wind and solar never generated enough energy to power anything substantial. They resorted to coal—easy, abundant coal. They mine it in secret."

I was dumbfounded. Burning coal and other fossil fuels was what polluted the air, which made us so sick. Or, maybe it didn't. After all the lies, I was not sure what to believe anymore.

"Mazie," I began.

Cutting me off, she said, "Jotham and his goons would have

nabbed you anytime. We had to go."

I did not know what to say. "I'm sorry," I mumbled.

"Don't be," she said, putting a hand on my shoulder. "You've been through a lot. We're going to help you survive out here."

"Who's we?"

"Whitetail."

She stopped walking. Her hand touched the rough rock wall. A keypad lowered. After entering a sequence, part of the rock parted and the keypad retracted.

We walked through the opening before it disappeared. "How does this work?" I asked, momentarily distracted.

"Geothermal energy."

The new tunnel brought us into a cave. Mazie turned off the flashlight. A faint light inched into the darkness. Like a moth to a light bulb, we avoided stalagmites as we climbed towards the light source.

When I followed Mazie through a narrow opening, I squinted as my eyes adjusted to the bright light. Blinking, I realized we were deep in the woods.

"Char told me Whitetail was a myth," I said, walking on whatever path Mazie chose.

She laughed. "He'd like to believe that," Mazie said.

"So, he's real?"

"Very." Mazie chose her steps carefully. "Just need to know where to look."

"Thought he found you."

"He does."

Mazie extracted a gun from her backpack. She looked over her shoulder often as we climbed the mountain from which we emerged.

"Take another step and you'll lose a foot," said a man's voice from behind me.

I froze.

"Is that anyway to greet an old friend, Douglas?" Mazie said.

Chapter 10

An old friend? He walked around us, pointing a large gun at us. His dark, thick beard hid his expression while his dark eyes scrutinized us through his scraggily, long, dark hair.

"Mazie?" he said. He took a couple of steps up the hill. "Who's the boy?"

"I'll explain inside," she said.

Douglas hesitated before lowering his gun. "You weren't followed," he added.

Mazie and I followed Douglas to a tree stump. Pressing somewhere on the side, he easily flipped the stump open as if it were on a hinge. The stump covered a dark hole.

Arms tucked in front of her body, Mazie jumped into the hole. Doing the same, I jumped in after Mazie. My body barely touched anything until I crashed onto the floor. Quickly, Mazie pulled me to the side, moments before Douglas landed exactly where I had fallen.

As I got off the floor, Mazie said, "Douglas, I want you to meet Xavier... Kelton."

Douglas' dark eyes looked from me to Mazie. He nodded as if he understood something.

"Xavier, this is the elusive Whitetail," Mazie told me.

Glancing around, I felt as though I had fallen through the rabbit hole into an underground hovel. The makeshift living area looked as disheveled as Douglas. The couch and table seemed to have been forgotten by the recluse.

"What's the problem?" Douglas asked.

He mostly had eyes for Mazie, although he kept quickly looking at me as if his eyes were rubber bands snapping back into place.

"Help him survive," said Mazie.

Before Douglas could answer, a ding echoed off the hovel's walls. Rushing over to one wall, he placed his hand on the wall. Green lights flashed above his hand, just like in the tunnel. The wall split in two, revealing a computer with multiple screens.

Pulling out a retractable seat, Douglas sat in front of his computer. After a few strokes on the smooth keyboard, he allowed the wall to swallow the computer.

"Just got wind of a prisoner transfer," Douglas told Mazie. He reached into a trunk, then started throwing black wads of material at me. "Change," he said, "you're coming."

Mazie relieved me of my backpack, then showed me to the bathroom to change. Before closing the door on me, she flipped a switch, bathing me in light.

Being away from it for a few days made me realize how much I missed electricity. I had no idea how it was possible, but I was grateful. It reminded me of home.

Dressed in black, I emerged from the bathroom. Without a word, Douglas handed me black gloves and a hat. Mazie nodded approvingly at me. Putting on the gloves, I followed Douglas through an opening.

He grabbed a small pack that was lying against the wall. "Outside," he said to me, "there is no verbal communication. I'm going to teach you the hand gestures I use. Pay attention. I'm only going to show them once."

Closed fist meant freeze. Open palm was wait. Look. Watch. Hide. Retreat. I hoped that I would remember them all.

We reached a green laser panel barricade. Stopping, Douglas placed his flashlight in his pack. "This is a one-way barricade," he told me. "Once we pass through, we cannot return this way. Anyone who tries gets electrocuted."

"How?"

"Point of use generator. My place is full of them," he said. "Now, we are wearing special gear. Once we put on the hats, we will be invisible to thermal imagery. Talking, however, renders it useless."

"Won't they be anticipating that?" I asked.

"Nope," he said stretching the knit hat over his dark hair. "It's unique nanotechnology—developed by your father." He pulled the hat over his face. Through the holes, his eyes told me that conversation was over and to do the same.

Pulling the hat down to my neck, I crossed through the barrier with Whitetail.

It felt surreal to walk through the tunnel, knowing my dad created what I was wearing. To know that he, in some weird way, was still protecting me gave me a sense of comfort that allowed me to cut through my fear.

The tunnel ended in a crack of an opening. Raising his hand, Whitetail told me to wait. He peered through the vegetation covering the crack.

Waving me on, we crept into the forest. The dense canopy kept the afternoon sunlight at bay. Behind some fallen trees, we met a couple who mirrored us in appearance. Using his hand signals, Whitetail communicated with them.

The four of us danced down the mountain. Seeing a road cutting a winding path through the forest, we found hiding places. We had not been spying on the road long when a low noise vibrated my eardrums. I had heard that noise before only in old movies.

On the deserted road, a dirty, beige truck drove into view. The lone man in the front only had eyes for the road in front of him. The back of truck looked like a big square box. I wondered what was inside.

Next to me, Whitetail began to scrape a twig on the side of a felled tree. The noises hurt my ears. The scraping stopped when a large deer strode down the mountain towards us. Whitetail jumped up with his arms stretched out wide. The deer sprinted towards the road.

I didn't want to look, but I couldn't tear my eyes away. Reaching the edge of the forest, the deer leapt onto the road.

The truck swerved left, crashing into a tree. I could barely see the driver slumped over the steering wheel. The deer pranced into the forest as the tree cracked on top of the large box, jarring the back door open.

Whitetail signaled to me to stay where I was. We watched the jarred door bounce a few times until it opened.

Two men jumped out of the truck. Their hands and feet were bound. One man pulled his shirtsleeves over his hands. Waddling to the front, he opened the door. I recoiled when he pulled a laser gun off the seat. He adjusted the setting, then shot at his feet. Partially free of his bonds, he shot the bonds off the second man. The second man, in turn, shot the final bonds off of the first man.

After returning the gun, the men looked around. Whitetail threw a rock down the hill. Without hesitation, they walked into the trees.

Whitetail and one from the other party met the men halfway. They gave the men hats and gloves. Reaching our hiding place, the now party of six split. Whitetail and I ran with the one man into the nearest opening in the rock. Holding a finger to his covered mouth, Whitetail told the man not to speak.

The stranger and I followed Whitetail through the natural tunnel. When darkness enveloped us, Whitetail opened a secure door into another natural tunnel. Dim wall lights followed us until we reached a fork. Tunnels branched in five directions. An underground stream trickled somewhere in the cave system. Whitetail pulled a series of levers cleverly disguised in the rough wall. A small hatch-like opening appeared on the wall near the ground.

Crawling through the opening, I felt as though I was inside a large ventilation system. We did not crawl long before Whitetail rolled through the side of the metal wall. The stranger and I followed his lead. I rolled out onto the floor of a long, cement tunnel lit by old fluorescent overhead lights. Like in the rest of the tunnel system, the lights followed us as we walked.

Stopping, Whitetail touched the wall. I stared into the vast tunnel, not knowing what was coming next. As soon as his hand disconnected with the wall, we were plunged into pitch black.

A hand grabbed my arm, pulling me towards something. My hands were placed on different round rungs of a ladder. A push told me to climb. The ladder swung as I climbed. When the swinging subsided, I assumed another person had joined me on the ladder.

My hands ran out of rungs to grab. Reaching around, I felt a smooth wall. The person beneath me grabbed my foot. Removing my foot from the rung, it found a floor. I stepped off the ladder then waited for further instructions.

Another body clumsily knocked into mine. After hearing something lock, dim lights pierced the darkness.

Whitetail waved us forward. Entering another tunnel, he lifted his facemask. "Sorry, only mine is equipped with night vision," he said.

Around a bend, the disheveled hovel came into view. The stranger walked into the hovel towards Mazie who sat on the couch. Taking off my hat and gloves, I handed them back to Douglas.

"Mazie?" the stranger said while ripping off his hat. His voice sounded as if he had not used it in a while.

Mazie slowly rose from the couch, looking as though she had seen a ghost. "Cal?" she said.

I crossed to the bathroom so I could change. Curiously, I turned to glance at the stranger's face.

"Xavier!" he called.

Chapter 11

I froze. Past the unkempt hair that curled around his ears and the short beard, I recognized him. "Dad?" I managed to say.

My vision blurred and my face felt wet. Dad hugged me. I did not want to let go.

"Thank goodness you got out," Dad said. "Where are Nickie and Mom?"

I looked at Dad from arm's length. "Nickie's in the town," I said. "Mom," I shook my head. My mouth did not want to finish the sentence.

"They got her, too," Dad said.

"Why?" I asked.

"Long story," Dad muttered. Rubbing his face, he sat on the couch. "Glad to see my technology still in use, Douglas," he said. "Thanks for taking care of my children, Mazie. I hope you have forgiven me after all these years."

"I was angry, Caleb," Mazie said as she sat in a nearby chair. She couldn't stop looking at Dad.

Dad, however, looked at everything. "Your style is distinctive, Mazie," he said. Turning to me, Dad said, "Your aunt built her first subterranean structure in abandoned coal mines under our grandmother's house."

"My aunt?" I said looking from Dad to Mazie.

"You didn't tell them?" Dad asked Mazie.

She shook her head.

I placed my head in my hands. I was not sure if I wanted to hear anymore.

"They were coming for him, Cal," said Mazie. "I wasn't going to let them take him like they took you."

Slowly, my head raised. "They took you?"

Closing his eyes, Dad sighed. When he opened them, his light brown eyes stared directly into mine. "It's time you heard the whole truth," he said.

"I was finishing grad school and applying for doctorate programs when they approached me. They, being the Society for Ecological Development under the larger umbrella fraternity, Sigma Epsilon Delta. They promised me guaranteed admittance to the program of my choice with a full scholarship. In exchange, I was to work on a few projects—'green projects.' I became a major contributing researcher on the one hundred percent recyclable project.

"Because of my research and development, I was invited to a major fraternal conference in Washington, D. C. There, I met people who all were in Sigma Epsilon Delta. Except, the E stood for different things like environmental, educational, and economic. I was sitting in a large conference room with the Greek letters plastered all over the place when I awoke.

"I was never an active member of the fraternity, so I never gave it much thought before then. In Greek, the symbols for Sigma and Epsilon resemble an S and an E. But, Delta looks nothing like a D. It's a triangle. In the scientific community, the Greek symbol, Delta, means change.

"Not long after that conference, fraternity members were being urged to stay away from non-members. I made my last visit home to say goodbye. My mom and dad understood that I needed to do what I could to protect the movement."

"What movement?" I asked.

"Your grandparents spearheaded the RR movement," Mazie explained. "Most people referred to it as the railroad or the second revolution."

"The RR stood for Redux Radix," Dad said.

"Stands," corrected Mazie.

"You and Douglas carried the torch?" Dad asked her.

"Someone had to," said Mazie. "You left us." Mazie sounded as if she wanted to cut Dad with her words. "When people started dying in the city en masse, we couldn't get a hold of you. I had no idea if you were alive or dead."

"Fraternity members were immunized," Dad said, "unknowingly. My wife, Sadie, found that out."

"Sadie a member, too?" Mazie asked.

"No," said Dad. "She is naturally immune. Sadie was studying microbiology at another university in the city. When they found her still living among the dying, they scooped her into the quarantine with us. Sadie always believed that she ended up with us because they found her useful."

"When the war apexed," said Mazie, "I hoped you were dead instead of fighting for the other side."

"I never fought for them," Dad said angrily.

"They protected you," spat Mazie. "You abandoned us!"

Dad stared at Mazie. "I'm sorry," he said softly. "I was trying to protect you from them. If that meant appearing as if I had abandoned you, then so be it."

Tears streamed down Mazie's face.

"I tried to do something from the inside," Dad added. "Not that I did much good. Thanks to Douglas, they did not have the chance to execute me."

"Who was the other man with you?" Douglas asked as he brought a tray of food.

"Don't know," said Dad. "We didn't talk about what we had done."

Douglas nodded.

Dad took a moment to eat some food before he continued. "When death walked through the streets, we were shipped to a quarantine facility. I spent the remainder of the war in quarantine, although they tried to drill into us that there was no war going on at all. They called it the devastation from ecological abuse. From the facility's large windows, I watched the city and surrounding area go dark. For weeks, I watched my beloved city burn from the modern glass skyscrapers to the nineteenth century stone beauties. After the embers darkened, I watched the bulldozers knock down whatever empty shells still stood. Not even a year later, I was watching them build the eco-pods and the electrical enclosure.

"When the New Era began, we were allowed to live in the new community—Pod City one-five," Dad continued. "Almost immediately, I became a leading scientist in the Nanotechnology Commission. I never forgot for what we were fighting, Mazie."

"I'm sorry, too, Cal," Mazie said. Her eyes were still damp. "What *did* you do?"

"Turns out there is a Population Commission," Dad said. "They are a very powerful commission and they do not like anyone trying to buck them." He took a swig from his glass. "All the plastic is recycled into soft weavable fibers. Every fiber is imbued with nanotechnology to be breathable and soft yet, durable and climate resistant. Somehow, the nanotechnology allowed the molecules to evolve, even mutate. The most common result was the strangulation of the user."

Maize nodded, probably remembering the shirt choking Nickie.

"They tried to pass it off as random wildlife attacks," Dad said. "From my research, I knew what was really going on. I tried to alert them about the issue. That was my first mistake. I was called in to see the district head of the Governing Commission. In his well-appointed mansion with the finest of Chinese goods on a hill above the Pod City, he tried to force my hand into working with them. I was offered a Global Card and I would get a set amount of Globals for each contribution to the population control effort. Needless to say, I turned them down.

"I was forced into the mines. After conspiring to start a few riots, they obviously thought that it was in their best interest to get rid of me. And, here I am."

"And Mom?" I asked.

"She confirmed my findings at her lab in the Biotech Commission," Dad said. "I was hoping the three of you would have gotten out before," Dad trailed off. "She's strong. You'll like her Mazie. Don't worry, Xav," Dad said, putting a hand on my shoulder. "Mom will be just fine. We'll get her."

"When?" I asked, hopeful.

"As soon as I formulate a plan."

"Plans take time," said Douglas. He gave my dad a look that I did not understand. "I'll open the dormitory for tonight."

After he left, Dad asked Mazie, "Did you and Douglas have any children?"

Mazie gazed in the direction that Douglas disappeared. "We never married," said Mazie.

"You two were so in love," Dad said, looking disappointed. "He showed me the ring."

"Plans change," said Mazie as her eyes met Dad's. "And so do people."

Dad said nothing more.

The dormitory held about two dozen bunk beds. The three of us chose beds. If Dad and his sister talked during the night, I had no inkling. I fell asleep immediately.

Douglas woke us when he turned on the lights. "Time to go," he said. "The truck was abandoned. It's only a matter of time before they start searching."

Urgency replaced grogginess. Douglas led us through a series of tunnels. When we finally emerged into the daylight, we had a full view of the town.

"Got a nice view of my house from here," Mazie mentioned.

Holding a pair of binoculars to his eyes, Douglas said, "The path to the house is clear. And, Mazie, don't worry about Jotham."

Chapter 12

Afaint smile flashed on her face before we trekked down the hill. When the trees began to thin on the edge of town, Mazie held us back.

"I'll open the back door," she whispered. "You two will run straight inside."

Dad gave Mazie a sharp nod. We watched her run across the lawn to the half-glass door. As soon as her fingers touched the doorknob, it opened. Dad pushed me in front of him. Together, we sprinted through the opened door.

In the kitchen, Mazie locked the door behind us. "Welcome home, little brother," she said. "I suggest getting rid of those Pod City clothes before I have to cut them off of you, too."

"Too?" asked Dad.

"Nickie," I said.

"You don't happen to have a lab?" Dad asked.

"No, but I can get you to one," said Mazie.

After showering, I found Dad, clean shaven, sitting with Mazie at the kitchen table.

"The most private lab would be in the old high school," Mazie said. "I don't think we should risk topside. It will be longer, but we should take the tunnels."

Mazie loaded a small bag with three guns, while extracting her flashlight and a small box. We took the same route through the basement that Char and I took to the generator. Before entering the hole under the chest, she gave Dad the flashlight. Opening the small box, Mazie removed a short stick. With a swipe against the side of the box, the stick erupted into fire.

She lit the lantern, then handed it to me. I climbed down first with the lantern. Dad followed. Then, Mazie jumped off the ladder, carrying the flashlight.

"Remember how to ride?" she asked Dad as she approached the bikes.

Laughing, Dad grabbed a bike.

Hanging my lantern on the same blue bike as before, I followed Mazie and Dad through the tunnel.

"I'm sorry that I never got to teach you how to ride a bike," Dad said. "Not having bicycles as transportation in the Pod Cities always struck me as odd."

We stopped at a door well before the generator. Setting the bikes against the wall, Mazie pulled paper out of her bag. She jotted down a note, then stuck it on the handlebars of her bike. Glancing at the note, I read, *H S lab*.

Opening the door, it revealed another tunnel.

"How does the flashlight run?" Dad asked. "All batteries would be dead by now."

"Modified Baghdad Battery," Mazie said with a wry smile.

"A what?" I asked.

"A Baghdad Battery uses a conductor, such as copper, a node, most likely iron, and an acidic electrolyte, like vinegar, to generate a small electrical charge," Dad explained. "They were found in archaeological excavations around the city of Baghdad and hail from ancient times."

"Cool."

An oval metal door signaled the end of the tunnel. Before turning the wheel, Mazie handed Dad and me guns. "We're entering the old subbasement," she said. "The old lab is two floors up. School is in session."

The subbasement was filled with old, broken junk. The dust was overwhelming, but I resisted the urge to sneeze. Dusty stairs took us to the basement. The squeaky door allowed us to pass more junk as we headed to the main staircase.

At the first landing, Mazie opened the door. Pausing, she listened. We tucked our guns under our crossed arms as we crept into the wide hallway.

Encountering no one, we entered the third door on the right.

Handing the bag to my dad, Mazie said, "I'll get what you need. Keep the door locked no matter what."

"Use our knock," said Dad.

Mazie smiled. Taking her gun, she left.

After locking the door, I asked, "Need any help?"

Dad rummaged through drawers and cabinets. "Find what you can and put it on this table."

We collected burners, beakers, test tubes, pipettes, gloves, and goggles from every corner and cabinet of the lab. Dad found all sorts of chemicals. He was setting up an area when we heard some tapping, two knocks, more tapping, and then, a soft kick on the door.

"It's your aunt," Dad said. "Let her in."

Opening the door, Mazie scooted inside. "The school is secure," she said. "Nickie is one floor up. Why don't you bring her down while we're waiting."

I tucked the gun into the front waist of my jeans, then pulled my shirt over to cover. Upstairs, I strolled down the empty hallway, peeking in empty classrooms.

"You want to say that to my face?" Nickie's voice carried down the hallway.

I no longer needed to slyly peer through narrow windows in the doors.

"You're nothing but Pod City trash," said another girl's voice. "I was telling Jett here that he shouldn't be going near you. Some of the filth could rub off. Goes for your brother, too. Shame he's cute."

My head poked inside the room in time to see Nickie bring her right arm back. Before I could reach her, Nickie's fist collided with a blonde girl's nose.

The blonde shrieked. She tried to cover her nose with her hand, but it could not stop the blood from trickling down her chin.

"Try to scrub off the contamination now, Jennara," said Nickie.

"Miss Exie!" Jennara sobbed.

A woman with short black hair clomped over in thick-heeled boots from working with another student. "Effective hit, Nickie," she said. "How's your hand?"

Jennara wailed for attention.

"Sorrel, take Jennara to get cleaned up," the woman dismissed.

Passing me, Sorrel glared while Jennara ignored my very existence.

"Fine, Miss Exie," Nickie said.

"Then, you've learned something," the woman said. Her green eyes pierced me. "You must be Xavier."

I nodded.

"I'm Exie," she said, holding out her hand.

She had a firm handshake. With the front of her hair sleeked to her jawbone and her dark pants tucked into her knee-high boots, she did not strike me as the teacher type.

"Nice to meet you," Exie said with a smile. I could tell she had already sized me up at first glance.

"And you. Can I borrow Nickie?" I said.

"You most certainly may."

Jett and Kai both had friendly looks for me as I waited for Nickie to gather her things.

In the hallway, Nickie asked, "What's up?"

Keeping Dad's arrival a secret, I said, "You'll see." As I led her down the stairs, I asked, "What was that about?"

"She's such a two faced," Nickie did not finish her sentence when she saw Mazie holding a door open for us.

Ducking inside, Nickie's bag slipped off her arm. Tears gushed down her cheeks as she ran towards Dad.

Dad's arms opened wide to receive his daughter.

"Daddy," Nickie cried.

I could not help but smile. Out of the corner of my eye, Mazie wiped her face.

"Where's Mom?" Nickie asked.

"We'll get her, Nickie," Dad said. "Don't you worry."

A knock on the door interrupted the reunion. Mazie opened the door for Char.

Char handed Dad a small cloth sack, saying, "Guess you ain't dead. Good." Turning to me, she said, "Brayden misses you. To say he is angry would be an understatement. He said, and I quote, 'If that scum, Jotham, crosses my path, he'll get what's coming to him.' Safe to say, you can return to the generator."

Glancing around the room, Char uncomfortably shifted her weight. "Speaking of returning," she began. Then, she abruptly left.

Dad advised us to sit a few rows back because of the chemicals. While he worked, Mazie kept an eye on the door. Nickie and I watched Dad drop cut pieces of our clothes into test tubes. We had never seen Dad work before. The Nanotechnology Commission frowned on lay people inside the labs. Around the dinner table, Dad would usually share his work with us. To see him heat mystery ingredients in a beaker, then drip carefully counted mccs into tubes was like getting to know my dad all over again.

Turning off the burners, Dad removed his gloves and goggles. "Nothing more to do than wait," he said. "Can I leave these untouched?"

"I'll have Exie lock the door," said Mazie.

When we exited the lab, we heard, "Oh, there you are, Mazie." Exie and Kai walked towards us.

"Could you lock the lab?" Mazie asked.

Exie pulled out a small metal ring filled with what looked like old style keys. Locking the door, she said, "We just saw some men carrying Jotham. I sent Jett to investigate."

"When will I be able to get back in there?" Dad asked.

Removing the key from the ring, Exie handed it to Dad. "Return the key when you're done."

The doors banged into the walls. Jett ran towards us. "Miss Exie," he said, "Jotham's dead."

Mazie fell into the wall behind her.

"How?" asked Exie.

"Don't know," Jett answered. "A trader found his body. They're taking him to the hospital for examination."

Standing again, Mazie asked, "Where did they find his body?"

"In a ditch on the side of the road," said Jett. "The trader said he was lying there like he'd been shot—he's seen plenty of those on the roads—but, there aren't any bullet holes."

"Are you sure?" Dad asked with interest.

Jett nodded. "I saw the body. There was nothing."

"What is it, Caleb?" Mazie asked.

"Lasers from a certain distance leave no trace except perhaps a microscopic scorch mark."

Nickie and I raised our eyebrows as we looked at Dad.

"I've seen these deaths," Dad said. Ignoring Jett's and Kai's shocked faces, Dad gasped. "The body needs to be checked for a mole."

"A mole?" asked Kai.

"A microcomputer comprised of thousands of nanochips," Dad explained. "Inserted into a person, its sole purpose is to record data. Then, when a receiver is in range, it will transmit its data."

"How far is its range?" Exie asked.

"No more than 20 meters," Dad said.

"Kai, let your mom know," instructed Exie.

Turning, Kai ran.

"Wait!" Dad shouted.

Kai stopped.

"When talking, it is best to keep at least two closed doors between you and the body," Dad said.

Nodding, Kai disappeared through the doors.

"You'll be at the house?" Exie said.

"Yes," said Mazie.

Exie swung her keys around her finger. "Jett, Nickie, we're done for today. Come, I want to lock the school."

Nickie looked from Exie to Mazie and Dad. "Where are you guys going?"

"The way we came," said Mazie.

"I want to go with you," Nickie said.

I understood Nickie's desire to not let Dad out of her sight again.

Mazie's hard eyes softened as she looked at Nickie. "I'm sorry Nickie, but you have to walk home. We don't know who we can trust out there."

Nickie's whole face fell, but she nodded.

"I'll walk you home, Nickie," Jett offered a little too eagerly for my liking.

Her eyes met his, then she smiled.

"I'll see you soon," Dad told her before we returned to the belly of the school.

As we entered the tunnels, Mazie asked, "What are you looking for, Cal?"

"Proof," said Dad, "that I did not make a mistake and put my family in harm's way."

Chapter 13

No one spoke during the return bike ride. Nor did anyone speak on the way into Mazie's house. Emerging from the basement, Mazie froze. Dad and I rushed to her side to see a man who I did not recognize fussing over pans on the stove.

"What are you doing in my house?" demanded Mazie.

"I used some of your sharp objects," the man said. "And I made dinner." He turned around, smiling at us. Without his wiry full beard and his long, mangy hair, I barely recognized Douglas. The glint in his dark eyes gave him away.

"How'd you get in?" asked Mazie, taking a few steps into the kitchen.

A door closed. "Dad?" called Nickie.

"I don't want to bog you down with the details," Douglas

said.

Dad moved in the direction of her voice. "I'm here, Nickie."

"Try me," said Mazie with one hand on her hip.

Turning off the stove, Douglas walked past Mazie into the sitting room. "Caleb," he said, "food is ready."

"Thanks, Douglas," Dad said.

My stomach growled at the smell of deliciousness. I met Dad and Nickie in the dining room. The oval cloth covered table was set for six.

"Why are you so upset to see me?" I heard Douglas ask Mazie in the kitchen.

She followed him into the dining room. "Did you kill Jotham?" Her voice was cold and flat.

Expressionless, Douglas placed platters of food on the table.

"Is that why you changed your look from wild animal to human being? So no one would recognize you?" Mazie interrogated.

"Do you really think of me that way?" Douglas asked in return.

"Yes or no?" Mazie demanded.

Douglas stared at her, then smiled. "I'm still the same man, Mazie," he evaded before disappearing into the kitchen. When he reappeared with more food, he said, "My plan was to use him and his contacts. He now being dead throws a wee little wrench into my plan."

Satisfied, Mazie joined us at the table.

While we ate, Nickie was formally introduced to Douglas and told a less detailed story of what had happened to Dad.

"Aunt Mazie?" Nickie said with wide eyes.

"No need for titles or prefaces," Mazie waved away. "Just Mazie is fine with me." She gave Nickie a warm smile.

After hearing a door close, Char ran into the room. "Sorry to intrude on this happy family reunion, but Exie just sent word from the hospital. They found scorch marks just like Caleb said. However, they have no idea how to find a microcomputer."

Dad chewed his lip as he thought. "Does the hospital have electricity?"

"Primitive at best," Char answered.

"I'll need a long fluorescent light, one or two bulbs should do, a microscope, enough battery power to run them both, and any wiring you can spare," Dad said. "Oh, and a small container made of lead."

"Love a good scavenger hunt," Douglas said, standing. He took a few steps towards the kitchen. "Coming, Charlotte?"

Perturbed, Char glared at him. After a breath, she said, "Of course, Dougy."

"Play nice," said Mazie. "We'll meet you at the hospital."

The basement door slammed.

"Douglas and Char never really got along," Mazie muttered. "Might as well clean up. I'll find more lanterns. We'll each need one in the tunnels."

"No," said Dad so sternly that Nickie and I stopped clearing the table. "We can't risk them finding out about the underground. Until that mole is destroyed, none of us are safe."

"That's if there's a mole," said Mazie.

"There is," Dad assured. Getting up, Dad helped clear the table.

Before we left, Mazie handed us all guns. "Is that necessary?" Dad asked, watching Mazie show Nickie how to use a small handgun.

"Being able to defend oneself is always necessary," Mazie said.

We headed outside with guns tucked under our clothes. Sticking close together, Mazie led us through a combination of worn streets and broken alleys. One tree-lined street ended at the crest of a hill. At the top of the hill, a parking lot separated us from the hospital entrance.

Grass and tall weeds grew through the cracks of the black top. As we reached halfway across the parking lot, a man jumped into our path. Pointing a gun at us, he said, "I'm not going to let you get away with it, Mazie."

"Get away with what, Justin?" Mazie said.

"Jotham's death," Justin answered.

"I didn't kill him," Mazie said. "Move aside." She sounded bored.

Justin snickered, then wiped his nondescript chin with a faded plaid sleeve. "Like I don't know what happened at your house. Couldn't kill him then. So, you and the boy disappeared. Funny how you just happened to show up once he's dead. Doesn't take a genius to put that together."

"No, it takes a moron."

"I don't like your tone," Justin sneered as he shook his gun.

"And I don't like your accusation," retorted Mazie, pulling her own gun from her waist.

Justin shook his head. "Stupid move." He motioned to another man pointing a much bigger gun at us.

My heart skipped a beat. I reached for my gun, but I hesitated to lift my shirttail.

"The lady said she didn't kill him," Douglas said, appearing behind Justin. He held a small black gun directly at Justin's head. "Now, unless you want to join Jotham in the hereafter, I would kindly suggest you and your friends head back to the stupid cave."

A shot echoed through the weathered parking lot. Douglas disappeared. Blood stained the broken pavement. Justin dropped before I heard another shot. The man with the big gun crashed into the weeds. Holding his gun steady, Douglas spun shooting above us. A body slammed to the ground beside me.

Lowering his gun, Douglas surveyed the three bodies littering the parking lot. "Always trigger happy," Douglas mumbled, shaking his head. His eyes met Mazie's. "Those two I killed in self defense."

Tucking her gun back into the waist of her pants, Mazie said, "I see that. Thank you." Without another glance at the carnage, she stepped past Justin's body.

Dad pulled Nickie close, trying to shield her from the vacant eyes staring into nowhere. Not wanting to dwell among the dead, we hurried into the hospital. Glancing behind me, I saw Douglas collecting the weapons off the ground.

He followed us inside, saying, "There were only those three goons." Securing his collection, he said, "We set an area up for you."

Douglas led us through the hospital to a set of double doors. On the other side of those doors, a large room greeted us filled with steel tables on wheels. All of the items Dad asked for and then some covered the tables. Oil lamps dotted every surface, eliminating shadows. Before Dad had a chance to touch anything, a door opened.

A petite woman walked towards Dad. "You must be the expert," she said. Gray streaks shone against her otherwise dark bun. "The body is many doors down. I am Doctor Phoebe Meltac," she added while she held out a hand.

Shaking it, Dad said, "Doctor, forgive me if I don't give you my name."

"What am I to call you?" asked Doctor Meltac.

With a wistful smile, Dad answered, "Doc."

"Okay, Doc, what's the procedure?"

"My team and I will put everything together. Once we find it, you will have to surgically remove it."

"I'll be standing by," Doctor Meltac said. She promptly left us to work.

Dad walked over to Mazie and Nickie then said, "Go somewhere safe. We'll see you soon."

"I want to help," said Nickie who did not want to be separated from us. "Please?" Her light eyes pleaded with him.

With a deep breath, Dad gave in. "Help," he told her, pointing at me.

Nickie helped me strip wires mainly by watching. We rigged the microscope and fluorescent light to run off of crude battery power. Fiberoptic cables connected the light to the microscope.

After securing everything on top of one table, Dad asked, "Where's the box?"

Char placed an ugly, dark gray box that fit perfectly in the palm of her hand on the table.

"Get Doctor Meltac," Dad instructed. When the doctor opened the doors, Dad told Mazie, Char, and Nickie, "Keep watch."

Douglas handed extra guns to the three of them before helping me push the table down the hall. The doors at the end opened easily for us. One table sat in the center of the small room. On top of that table laid Jotham covered only by a thin sheet. We pushed the machine to where Dad indicated. Across the room, Doctor Meltac uncovered a cart full of shiny tools. She and Dad stripped off the sheet, exposing nakedness I never wanted to see.

Holding the light at each end, Douglas and I waited for Dad's signal. With Dad's eyes firmly resting on the microscope's eyepieces, he waved at us.

Douglas flipped the switch. Slowly, we inched the light over Jotham's body. Per Dad's instructions, we kept it about five centimeters above his skin. I tried not to look down as my feet shuffled to the side. We raised it to pass the light over his plump mid-section when Dad signaled for us to stop.

Searching for the exact source of the light distortion, we spent much too much time moving the light back and forth and from side to side over the one area I wanted to ignore. Doctor Meltac drew a small box on the left side of his body. Finishing our light scan, Dad found no other distortions.

As soon as Doctor Meltac picked a sharp object off her cart, I averted my eyes. However, I had no idea where to look. My eyes searched the dark corners of the room. The only light illuminated the dead guy. My fingers wrapped themselves into the hem of my shirt. I wished that I would be able to unhear the squishing. Shifting my weight from foot to foot did not distract me.

A dull thunk signaled relief. Carrying the ugly gray box, Dad led us out of the room.

Outside the door, Doctor Meltac said, "So that good-for-nothing Mayor was a mole?"

"We'll soon find out," said Dad.

Mazie, Nickie and Char met us in the hall.

"This needs to be hooked up to a computer," Dad said.

"Generator," said Char.

Doctor Meltac opened a panel in the wall. "With three dead outside the hospital," she said while pulling out a lever, "my daughter, Kai, will take you below." After closing the panel, she walked us to a staircase. Kai stopped on a landing below us when her mother opened the door.

"Mom?"

"Take them through to the generator."

Kai waited for us to reach the landing before she led us down more flights of steps. Stopping on a doorless landing, she opened a hatch in the floor that revealed a second staircase.

"Keep going down till the stairs stop. I'll be right behind you," Kai said.

Char and Dad descended first. Nickie crept next. I followed Nickie with Mazie and Douglas behind me. Little orange lights illuminated every third step. The sound of the hatch locking reverberated in the narrow stairway.

My tired legs got a respite when the stairs gave way to a wide tunnel. Waiting for Kai, I noticed more orange lights.

Kai stepped off the last step. Walking past us, she said, "This way."

Navigating the maze of corridors and rooms, Kai explained, "The hospital has a very large underground shelter. Minimal back-up generators keep these emergency lights on."

When the lights ended, the tunnel was plunged into an empty darkness. Kai grabbed a lantern off the wall. Lighting a stick, she shared it with Char who lit her own lantern. Douglas switched on his flashlight. We kept a brisk pace through the tunnel until we reached an oval metal door. Mazie turned the wheel that opened the door to the main bunker.

"We can reach the generator from here, Kai, if you wish to return," said Mazie.

"Can I come with you?" Kai asked quietly.

"Of course you can," Dad said.

Once we stepped over the threshold, Mazie and Char turned different wheels, closing one door and opening another.

The opened door led us to the generator's prep room. Carrying a mug, Brayden strolled towards us. "What's the meaning of this? Who are all these people?" he asked.

"We need the computer, Brayden," said Char calmly.

"Hmpf," grunted Brayden as he led us into the generator's main floor.

"Once this box is opened," Dad said, "no more talking. Xavier, you will wire this microcomputer directly to the generator's computer."

Nickie and Kai stared at the massive generator in wonder. Handing me the box, Dad said, "Extract all the information."

Box in one hand and flashlight in the other, I scooted under the control panel. "Opening the box," I announced.

Perching the flashlight, my fingers pried open the lid. The mostly black kidney shaped mole fell into my hand. Turning it over in the light, I examined it. I disconnected wires from the control panel, then reconnected the microcomputer between them. Pulling myself out from under, I depressed the on switch. A few strokes on the keyboard filled the room with sound.

A male voice said, "Insert this into your outside contact. These new moles have a three hundred meter transmission radius, so it doesn't matter where it goes. In a few days, a recon drone will patrol the area."

"Yes, sir," said another man.

A door closed. Heavy footsteps were the only sound.

"Got the coal?" the same man's voice asked.

"Yeah," said a young man's voice. "Ready to meet this scum?"

Two doors slammed.

"I don't know why we bother with those savages," the young man said. "The wild will get them all eventually."

"The problem is that we don't know how many there are or how advanced they are. We don't even know where they are," the man answered. "The drone will track the mole, collect its information, then command will retrieve it. Command will be able to assess the threat and determine the best way to proceed."

A door opened.

"Shouldn't we wait in the rover?" the young man asked.

After a door slammed, another door opened then closed.

"Where is he? I thought he'd be here by now," the young man said after a while of silence.

"You're late," the older man's voice shouted.

"We don't all have the luxury of powered transportation," said a new voice.

Mazie recoiled.

"I don't have time for this, Jotham," the man said. "Do you have the information?"

"Let me see it," Jotham demanded.

"After all this time, you still don't trust me," said the man.

Something heavy slammed into the ground.

"Self preservation is on the top of my list," said Jotham.

"The information," the man said sounding annoyed.

"My men are working on snatching an escapee," Jotham said. "And, I got wind of a transport heading northward. I'll have more details next week."

I heard shuffling.

"Hey, what gives?" Jotham asked.

"Stun him," the man ordered.

Static distorted the sounds.

"Last bit of coal we'll ever give you," the man muttered. "Don't want to be here when he comes to."

More static muffled the voices.

"Let's go!"

Two doors slammed.

Brayden gasped. "It has rendered a three dimensional map, seeing through walls and everything."

"Destroy it!" said Dad.

Chapter 14

I climbed under the control panel. Unhooking it from the control panel, I connected the mole to the short. I barely got my hands away before the microcomputer burned bright orange. With a series of pops and a strong stench of burnt silicon, the mole died. Using my sleeve, I removed it, dropping it quickly into the lead box.

Dad took the box from me as I emerged. Securing the lid, he said, "This needs to be welded shut."

Taking the box, Brayden disappeared.

"We need to ring the warning bells," said Mazie.

"They don't work," Brayden yelled.

"Have to use the old church bells," said Char. She too disappeared.

"Drones," Douglas said. His face wore a pensive look. "I'll

be generous and give us a day to prepare and stock up on supplies."

Char returned to the room, saying, "I told security." She glanced at Mazie. "So, it looks like Jotham was killed by accident."

"I don't think so," Dad said. "We heard static twice. Only an electrical disturbance would cause static."

"The laser gun," I said.

"Yes. It was fired twice—once to stun him and once to kill him."

"Why?" asked Nickie.

"We might never know," said Douglas.

"People are gathering," Brayden yelled from another room.

They began to leave. "Wait," I said, causing everyone to look at me. "If the mole is destroyed, then it can't emit a tracking signal. Does that mean the drone won't come?"

"It'll come," said Douglas. After taking a sweeping glance of the generator, he returned to the prep room.

"Dad," Nickie said in a small voice, "I'm scared."

Throwing a comforting arm around her, he reassured, "It will be okay."

I followed them to the main room where the townspeople had begun to gather. Mazie addressed the group, telling them about Jotham and the drone.

"I thought they lost control over the last of the functioning satellites?" asked a man in the crowd.

"They did," Douglas said.

"Then how are they going to control a drone?"

"Nanotowers," Dad offered. "Nanotowers are embedded

into each Pod City perimeter and high speed rail lines. In essence, they can program the drone to fly from nanotower to nanotower. New instructions can be given at each nanotower."

A voice in the crowd quietly asked, "Who's in charge now that Jotham is gone?"

"I am," said Exie, walking through the crowd. "We don't want to be detected by that drone. Follow emergency procedures. Fill the stores with as much as possible as quickly as possible. Remember an active bunker system keeps all doors open."

As fast as Exie could bark orders, people took them. Exie put people in charge of food, lanterns, beds, children, first aid, and general traffic. Families helped other families. Metal doors opened corridors and new rooms. Every person had a job.

"Miss Exie?"

"Yes, Jett?"

"What should I do?" His eyes scanned the people.

"You're parents kept emergency supplies." Exie's tone softened when she spoke to him. "Bring everything you can, then meet me in the war room."

Exie turned a wheel along the wall opening a door. "Mazie, bring your group."

While Kai left us to help her mom, we followed Exie through the opened door. After closing the door, she called, "Doctor Kelton."

Dad nodded. "Caleb."

Exie walked around the large central table so that she was facing the door. "Congratulations, Caleb, you are our official Pod City expert." She changed her focus onto Douglas. "Who are you?"

"Corporal Douglas Sheridan. But, you might know me better as Whitetail."

Exie's eyebrows raised. "Sit," she said. As metal chairs scraped against concrete, Exie continued. "I'm going to keep this short. Mazie, you are second in command. We need to get this generator up and running as quickly as possible. Anyone able to should be in there. Since Brayden would be happy to do it all himself, Char, you take whom you see fit. Mazie, get what you need from your house. I'm going to oversee our weapons cache."

Someone knocked on the door. "Come in, Jett," Exie said. When he poked his dark head inside the door, Exie rose from the table. "Let me show you where to put your things, then I'm putting you to work."

"Cal, Nickie, can you help?" Mazie asked.

They nodded.

"Guess that means that Xavier and Douglas are with me," said Char.

Escaping the busyness of the main room, we entered the generator room. Its constant hum soothed my nerves. Without his usual ornery antics, Brayden put Douglas and me to work. After encircling the generator at least once, Dad and Mazie joined us.

When the lights reached full luminosity, Exie came to bask in our hard work. "Brayden, give me a full report of our facilities as soon as possible."

"Yes, ma'am," Brayden said with a salute.

After showering in the bunker's expansive men's bathroom, Douglas, Dad and I returned to the war room. Jett joined us at the table.

"What's the plan, General?" Douglas asked Exie. "Are we hiding or are we shooting it down?"

"If we shoot it down, they will most certainly attack us. We wouldn't stand a chance. It is best if they do not know we are here," Exie answered.

"If we joined with other settlements, we could attack them," Douglas suggested.

Exie studied Douglas for a moment. "We're still at a disadvantage against their equipment. Their weapons are too advanced; we have no defense against them. Real outside help would be needed."

"The closest is Quebec," said Char.

Douglas shook his head. "They've been struggling for decades ever since they broke away from Canada. Buying Maine, New Hampshire, and Vermont hasn't given them the boon they had hoped for."

"What about Canada?" inquired Char.

"No good," Douglas said. "They're secretly helping Alaska fight the Chinese while trying to keep China from invading their southern border."

"If it's so secret, how do you know?" Char asked with her eyebrow raised.

"I know these things." Taking a breath, Douglas continued, "The border with Texas is still heavily watched. Anything from Cuba would take too long to get through the swampy wasteland that used to be Florida."

"So, we're on our own?" said Char.

Douglas did not answer.

We all knew the answer was yes. The Pod Cities' Protector Units had better equipment, better transportation, and better communication. We relied on centuries old technologies or broken and unreliable equipment.

I wanted to sink in my chair, wallowing in hopelessness until Nickie asked, "How did all this happen? I mean, why are we out here, all alone, without the comforts that the people in the Pod Cities enjoy?"

"That's a long, convoluted story," said Exie, leaning back in her chair.

"Please, Miss Exie," Nickie pleaded.

Taking a deep breath, Exie began, "Okay. But, I'm only going to give you a broad history. Everything that led to this moment could fill volumes. You have to realize that there is no one culprit. The blame can be spread in multiple directions. To give you a better background, I'm going to start in the early 1900s. In 1913, the Federal Reserve Bank was created and the United States implemented a federal income tax. Money began to be regulated under central control. Then, in 1929, the stock market crashed which caused the Great Depression. The country remained in the Depression until we entered World War II in 1941."

"What does this have to do with now?" asked Jett. "That was so long ago."

"Because our decline was a slow one, not unlike the fall of the Roman Empire," Exie answered. "When the war ended in 1945, we paid to rebuild war-torn Europe and forgave debts owed to us. Then, we entered the Cold War—technically, a nuclear weapons building race, which lasted until 1991.

"Wars aside, over the years, the government cozied up next to lobbyists who represented big corporate interests, as well as many other organizations and private people. Laws were passed and money was spent on things that were not in the public's interest. Even when the public ardently disagreed, power-hungry politicians, who were supposed to represent the people, decided that they knew better than their constituents and passed laws that hurt the people. With the advent of globalization, companies, organizations and some wealthy individuals spent more and more money buying politicians. These politicians, in turn, made things easier for those people in spite of everyone else.

"While all of this was happening, labor unions stopped representing their members. For decades, they bullied not only the workers, but also the companies for whom they worked. Through all of their demands, they gouged their employers, both private and public. Labor unions morphed from a protecting institution to political shills—doing the bidding of their favored elected official.

"The Federal Reserve removed the dollar from being the gold standard in 1971. Not having our dollar backed by gold caused massive inflation. As the prices of everything rose, the Federal Reserve did nothing to stop inflation although they claimed to be doing so. Over the years, the dollar lost its value against other currencies. Countries with no currency of their own used to use the U. S. dollar. Eventually, they stopped using it, causing the dollar to devalue further.

"Concurrently, a progressive political movement, under the guise of being for the people, bullied its way across the country.

It called for things like social justice, economic equality, and everyone giving his or her fair share. Legislation widened the scope of federal education standards, environmental protection assurances, welfare programs, federal housing and education loans, and instituted national health insurance mandates."

"How were those bad things?" Jett asked.

"In the abstract, those things sound like good ideas," Exie explained. "But, when implemented, they stripped people's individual liberties and erased the sense of personal responsibility. In education, for example, laws were made to favor teachers' unions instead of the students. On every level, education became more about indoctrination than learning. Students were punished for having an idea different than what they had to regurgitate. Parents slowly lost control over their own children's education. The government was setting course to control every aspect of people's lives. They, directly or indirectly, controlled what the people bought, how they traveled, what they ate, what they watched, what they read, and how much money they made. And, all these government-expanding programs cost money— more money than the country could sustain."

"How, how did people allow this to happen?" Nickie asked quietly.

Exie sighed. "Not having to think for oneself is easier. Many believed that they were entitled to everything for nothing. They accepted the partial picture that they were given. Questioning was discouraged. A lowest common denominator society was encouraged. Once enough people followed like mindless sheep, trying to make them see and think for themselves became virtually impossible. From an increasingly expanding government to large heartless private organizations, they all took advantage of the seemingly ignorant and apathetic public.

"Our traditions, values, morals, and ethics eroded until there was nothing left. Some people tried to preserve. The media created, yet, government controlled, culture would not allow it. Preservationists went to ground. The people began to protest. They protested the superfluous spending, the excessive wars, the intrusive projects, and the idea that someone else made decisions for them.

"The government paid no attention to them. The media demonized the protestors, calling them crude names and tried to silence them with horrific labels. When the movement began changing elections, voter fraud reached new heights. Not only did the dead vote, but so did non-citizens, mostly illegal immigrants, and fictitious people. They did everything to keep their power.

"Everything also included a new round of protests. These protesters were a different breed. Some had valid grievances, but the protests were coerced by seemingly invisible hands. Centrally controlled and well organized, they invaded every major city in all fifty states, when we still had fifty states. Although the protests suffered from infighting and disease, they used it to their advantage. Riots erupted in every protest city.

"When the violence escalated, city police forces could no longer control them. Armed citizens began defending their shops, homes and families. At first, mayors and governors called in their state's National Guard. Then, the President of the time intervened. He implemented martial law across the country."

"What is martial law?" Nickie asked.

"That is when the armed forces come in as the police force," Exie explained. "The armed forces are controlled by the President as Commander-in-Chief. Local authorities no longer had any say. The federal government became the central source of power in the country.

"The rioting subsided. Martial law, however, did not vanish. The federal government set up security checkpoints. Every person, regardless of age, was issued an electronic national ID card."

"Those should have never been allowed," interrupted Douglas. "The states already issued photo IDs and driver's licenses. The little plastic cards gave the states too much control over our lives as it was." Douglas shook his head in disgust. "Anything a person gives for what they perceive as a little more security always squashes them in the end. No government, local or national, should ever have had their grimy little hands in so many things—especially with such direct effect on the people's everyday lives."

Exie continued, "The cards, embedded with global positioning tracking, had to be shown everywhere and carried at all times. Those who did not comply were jailed. Streetlights and drones monitored everyone. They watched every movement and listened to every conversation, even from behind closed doors and inside private homes. Privacy was a thing of the past.

"Of course, all that monitoring was expensive. Tax rates soared. Those who could afford it abandoned the country. Before the Global was adopted as the new world currency in 2018, China began to cash in their U.S. bonds. To pay on the bonds, the government resorted to selling its territories. They sold the Pacific islands to Japan and Indonesia. Great Britain bought the Virgin Islands, while Cuba acquired Puerto Rico. Unfortunately, the monies from those sales were not enough to pay back China."

"Why did the government owe money to China?" asked Jett.

"Because of decades of spending more money faster than they could 'earn' it, the U.S. ran out of money. With a deficit in the double digit trillions of dollars, they looked to foreign governments as loan sources. China was our biggest foreign lender. And, they happened to be growing their own economy as well as military might," Exie said. "A society full of entitlement programs costs money. Those government programs chose to whom they gave entitlements. Some genuinely needed them, many did not. Entitlements were given as favors and some were taught how to milk the system to get more and more of the seemingly infinite supply of money as they raised the debt ceilings higher and higher. Plus, they gave what they considered aid to a multitude of foreign countries.

"Eventually, China demanded Hawaii in lieu of cash payment. By 2020, one state down, the United States had officially defaulted. Debtors were knocking on the proverbial door. The countries to whom money was owed, wanted to carve up the country for themselves. With Quebec buying the northeastern states, all but China had been staved.

"In 2021, Texas seceded. Completely broke, the government could not stop them. Shaking off all the oppressive regulations of the previous decades, the Republic of Texas flourished. People began to flock into Texas in search of jobs, prosperity, and a new found liberty. It re-ignited the people's desire to revolt against the oppressive collusion of government and what industry was left.

"To quell the revolt, the military was sent to the border with Texas. When people and goods could no longer flow freely over the border, the revolt quickly ran out of money and supplies. So, however, did the government.

"The Global made everything much more expensive then even the withering dollar did. The U.S. still could not pay back China's loans and the compounding interest. China wanted the debt clear. When debt forgiveness negotiations failed with the Chinese, Alaska seceded to save themselves from being handed over to China.

"Canada closed the border in 2024 months before China took the western United States to the Rocky Mountains. Afterwards, China deemed the debt settled.

"The new, smaller Unites States acted like nothing ever happened. They reverted to their favorite tactic—environmental blackmail. New taxes were levied while new laws were enacted."

"Why, though?" Nickie asked.

"Control," Mazie answered.

Exie nodded. "It is easier to control the people when they feel guilty for their actions."

"I still don't understand," said Nickie. She looked from Mazie to Exie. "Why control people? Why couldn't they just leave people alone?"

Smiling at Nickie, Exie explained, "To a truly independent spirit like yours, you will never be able to understand the lust for power and control."

As Nickie processed, Exie continued, "Their environmental blackmail came to a head when an extremely active hurricane season devastated Florida. With the economy in shambles, neither private nor public could afford to rebuild. The entire Floridian peninsula had been abandoned within five years.

"The government told people that we could not stay dependent on non-renewable energy sources. Solar and wind farms had already been in use, but with the coaxing of the government, they drove the last of the coal, natural gas and petroleum providers out of business.

"Every single item that was sold was electrical in one way or another. Outside the cities, people held on to their old non-electrical equipment. The increase in electrical output caused a strain on the power grids. Rolling brown and black outs became commonplace. Due to a lack of fuel, people found it hard to survive winter. Hot summers and localized pandemics killed even more people.

"Thousands died each year from lack of energy or food or medicine. Many of the sick were turned away for treatment because their lives weren't deemed important. The Redux Radix movement started and caught on like wildfire.

"Uprisings began as waves. Legislation censored all internet content. Groups over ten were cut down by the riot police. Soon, we were fighting a full-fledged civil war. The government, however, fought dirty. Many in the military deserted to help fight with their families. They bombed our homes and businesses using drones. We hacked into their system."

"That's how we discovered how many people had been detained at Guantanamo Bay over the decades," Douglas added.

"What do you mean?" asked Nickie.

"Before it was abandoned in 2054, Guantanamo Bay was a naval base on the island of Cuba. Originally, it was used as a fueling station. In 2002, it became a detention center for foreign terrorists with whom the government could do nothing else. A decade later, Americans were allowed to be detained there. Whomever the Department of Homeland Security deemed to be a 'home-grown terrorist' was sent to rot there without due process. The Government continued to broaden their definition of terrorist," explained Douglas with disdain in his dark eyes. "In the decades that followed, many people disappeared from their daily lives never to be found. The number of detainees at Gitmo, as it was called, was never disclosed. We only found out after the deep security hack of 2052."

"If only the people had kept their elected officials in check. Made them represent the people who elected them instead of allowing them to be so self-serving. Maybe, just maybe, none of this would have happened," said Mazie.

"Constitution preservation should have been the most important issue," Exie agreed. "Those who wanted to preserve what the original document upheld were silenced. The masses were told that the Constitution was too old and irrelevant. That was the furthest thing from the truth."

"A youth-obsessed culture disregards anything old," Mazie added.

Exie nodded. "Liberty should always be preserved. To do that, a free society needs constraints on their government—keeping their power and scope limited. *That* is the essence of the original U.S. Constitution."

We sat silent. Nickie and I had never heard of such things. Even Jett did not seem to know all the details.

Breaking the silence, Exie continued, "For a while, we were winning the fight. Then came the electromagnetic pulses. Luckily, we had been learning how to survive without electricity. We did not give up. Their final act was to use biological warfare against us.

"The dead were not counted. Whomever they did not 'save' were left to fend for themselves. And we have. We have survived on determination, ingenuity and scrounging."

Listening to Exie's story, I was shocked but not surprised. I knew the fabrication they taught us in school. I also knew how the Pod Cities operated.

"What if we leveled the playing field?" I asked.

"How?" asked Exie.

"If I could get us access to their system, could we monitor it?" I looked directly at Douglas while asking my question.

"I could," Douglas muttered. "We would need a secure frequency and—"

"It would be too dangerous," interrupted Dad. "You would need to have physical access to do what you're saying Xavier."

"Yes," I began, "I'd have to hardwire—"

"No!" Dad's voice was stern.

"Dad," Nickie said quietly, "how else are we going to get Mom?"

"I'll think of a way," Dad said.

"Caleb," said Douglas, "we might not have another way."

Dad looked from face to face, desperately wanting someone to give him an alternative plan.

Placing a hand on Dad's hand, Nickie said, "We got this far."

"Someone else," Dad said.

"No one knows the Electric Commission like I do," I said.

Dad knew that I was right. He also knew the risk. Furrowing his brow, he frowned. Dad's brow always furrowed when he thought hard. Nickie and I knew that as a sign to not bother him.

"We prepare in the morning," Dad finally said.

Chapter 15

Leaving the war room, Char led us through a series of tunnels. The final metal oval door revealed a cozy sitting room. The giant puffs of color floating on top of the hard floor begged me to flop into one. To my dismay, we walked through the sitting room into a hallway filled with more oval metal doors.

After passing a few doors, Mazie said, "This was built to act as more of a long term type of housing." As we passed another door, she said, "My room."

Stopping at the next door, Mazie pushed a small protrusion in the middle of the door. A keypad appeared on the wall. Entering a code, she said, "Caleb, I knew that when you returned you would need a place to stay."

Dad gave his sister a warm smile as she opened the door. Not entering his room, Dad walked with us.

Nickie got the next room, then I. My room was the first room I saw when Mazie opened the door. Choosing one of the two single beds, I surveyed the room. Above the two beds were another two folded into the wall. A long desk area had two chairs. Across from the desk was a tall chest. On the last wall, a row of doors indicated a wall of closets.

"Knock, knock," said Nickie.

Nodding her in, she sat on the other bed.

"My room is exactly the same," she told me. "Char and Douglas each have their own rooms, too. Douglas did protest a little saying that he should be in a different room. I wonder what he meant by that." Pausing for a moment, she leaned towards me. "Do you think we have a chance of getting Mom out?"

Remembering accessing the mainframe from my bedroom in PC one-five, I said, "As long as I can still get in undetected."

"Of course you can," Nickie said as she leaned back. "You've had loads of practice." She threw me a mischievous smile, then left me to sleep.

During a breakfast of leftovers, I asked, "What's the plan?"

"I need to check my work in the lab first thing," Dad said. "Could I bother you to take me, Mazie?"

"Sure."

"Afterwards, we'll discuss," Dad assured me.

Leaving our private bunker, Mazie took Dad one way while Char took us another.

"Where's Douglas?" Nickie asked.

Without looking around, Char said, "Who knows. He's a

weird one."

"In what way?" asked Nickie.

"I'll just say that he spends too much time alone in those mountains."

"Have you known him long?" Nickie inquired further.

"Not as long as I've known Mazie."

"How long have you known Mazie?"

Char glanced at Nickie with a small smile. "I met Mazie during the war," she said. "After my fiancé was killed in the battle of Durham, I packed a bag and left for parts unknown. While I was wandering, I stumbled upon a subterranean construction site. They needed help, so I offered my skills. Mazie was the architect. When that job finished, I followed her to the next job. We became friends. It's hard not to bond over losing loved ones to war." Her brown eyes sparkled with emerging tears. "Anyway, when the war finally ended, I had nowhere to go. No home to where I could return. There wasn't anyone left who made it feel like home." Char took a small breath. "Mazie invited me here. I have made this my home."

"How did you meet Douglas?" Nickie asked.

"He just showed up at the house one day. Mazie was so excited to see him. However, the war had scarred him. As suddenly as he had arrived, he left. Broke Mazie's heart. I only saw him one other time before his recent arrival."

Char said nothing more about Douglas. Surprisingly, Nickie did not ask.

The door leading to the main bunker was open. People scurried, carrying items from one place to another. Seeing the lights still on, I felt pride in my handiwork.

"Char," said Exie beckoning her into the war room. "You two, too."

Glad to be included, we followed Char into the war room. Brayden was already sitting at the table with a stack of papers.

As we sat, Exie said, "Your report, Brayden."

"Anything above ground is completely inoperable. I don't know if the stations will ever be fully functional again."

"We need eyes up there," Exie said.

"The diagnostic revealed what I think are periscopes."

"How many?"

"Eight," said Brayden. "I believe there is also a com center that can be linked into our main communication system."

"Take us," Exie said.

Brayden's beady eyes searched his papers. Scratching his coarse white beard, he said, "I don't know how to get there."

"Mazie might know," Char suggested.

"I might know what?" Mazie asked while entering the room with Dad.

"Where the other command center is," said Brayden.

Sitting down at the table, Mazie said, "This bunker was built before my time. I've only... added on." She let out a barely audible gasp. "I'll be back. Nickie, can you come with me?"

Nickie nodded her head.

"Wait," said Dad. He looked at Nickie and me. "Someone tampered with my work. That's why the shirt...." Not finishing his sentence, Dad placed a hand on Nickie's. "I'm sorry I couldn't stop it."

Nickie gave Dad a hug, then left with Mazie.

"Come in, Doctor," said Exie looking out the door.

Doctor Meltac entered the war room with her daughter, Kai. "The bunker medical facility is fully operational. Do you need anything else?"

"Thanks, Phoebe," Exie said warmly. "See Jett about weapons."

As they left, Exie said to Brayden, "How about a scope?"

"I found the entrance to one," Brayden said, looking excited. "I'll fetch my lantern."

While we waited for Brayden, I asked Dad, "How did someone tamper with your work?"

Dad sighed. "I designed the technology to virtually eliminate the need for different clothes for different seasons."

As we followed Brayden through deserted tunnels, Dad continued, "Initially, I thought there was something wrong with my formulas. What my little lab experiment proved was that someone added to my formula."

"What did they add?"

Although we were two closed doors away from the main bunker, Dad looked around before answering. "Nanolife," he whispered.

Exie stopped. Turning to face us, she said, "Nano-what?"

"Nanolife," Dad repeated. "It was supposed to be an energy independent machine. The concept has been thrown around in the scientific community for over a century. I heard rumors about its development for decades. However, what was achieved bends scientific ethics so far they cease to exist." Dad ran his fingers through his longish light brown hair. "Instead of a self-charging battery, it is an evolving life form. And, it's reproducing. The attacks happen because it's fighting for the survival of its kind. Being nano, it can spread everywhere and change everything."

"Sounds like one of those old science fiction movies with the rise of the killer machines," said Char.

Dad gave her an anything is possible look, then said to me, "We start as soon as Douglas returns."

Exie took her eyes off Dad, then continued walking. Reaching the end of the lighted corridor, Brayden's lantern poorly cut the darkness.

"Why isn't this part lit?" asked Exie.

"Not connected to our grid," Brayden said. "I don't know how to turn it on."

He shone his lantern into a curved niche. "Here it is."

Giving the lantern to Char, Brayden turned a dark metal wheel on the floor of the niche. A round metal hatch tilted open. "Watch your step," he said as he pointed the light down the hole.

Our feet echoed on the metal rungs. Reaching the bottom, we stood in the relative darkness before Brayden joined us.

Brayden's feet barely touched the floor before he groped the wall. Dim lights kept the shadows in the corners of the small room. Some type of electrical equipment filled one wall while a metal column hung from the ceiling in the center of the room.

"This stuff's gotta be over a hundred years old," Char said, running her fingers along the equipment.

"Does the periscope still work?" asked Exie.

Brayden released handles on the sides of the column. Putting her hand on the handles, Exie pressed her eyes on the column.

"Oh my," Exie trailed off as she turned around with the column.

Lights on the electrical wall came alive. Then I heard, "Scopes, this is Command. You are online." Nickie's voice sounded so far away.

Curiously, I pressed a large black button next to a long, thin protrusion. "Hello, Command," I said. "This is," I saw the number five inscribed on a panel, "scope five. Thanks so much."

"Xavier?" Nickie asked through the speaker.

"Yes."

"Mazie wants to know if everything works."

"Tell her unbelievably well," said Exie.

I relayed the message.

"Mazie is coming to you now," said Nickie.

"Thanks, Nicks."

Moving my attention away from the microphone, I noticed Char examining one of the screens. Mostly dark, a greenish line originating in the center of the screen swept a constant circle.

"This has to be an old radar screen!" Char said.

"Wonder if it works," Dad said, looking over her shoulder.

Still turning the scope every which way, Exie said, "We need to get these things manned. Two people per station. Brayden, you can train."

Footsteps on the ladder tore Exie away from the scope. Taking a quick look around, Mazie walked towards me. She pushed the button, saying, "We're coming your way Nickie."

"Okay," said Nickie.

Climbing out of the hatch, the corridor was lit by the same single bulbed, metal pendant lights that lit the scope room.

While we walked, Mazie explained, "We are walking through the original bunkers constructed by the U.S. military. After coal mining in this area stopped, the underground chambers were converted into this bunker system. The main entrance was through the armory. From what I gathered, sometime in the late 1960s it was mostly abandoned and it was sealed in the early 1990s.

"Sporadic coal mine to bunker conversion started privately in 2002 and 2003. Over the next fifty years, it grew to what we have now. This century's construction was mainly fallout shelters. Whereas last century's construction was more defensive.

"I came across the original blueprints when I was planning the bunker under my house. In all the chaos and what not, I forgot to return them."

Exie gave Mazie an of-course-you-did look with a wry smile.

Two direct corridors later, we entered a large multileveled round room. Steps led to the lower levels, but we crossed a narrow bridge to the center where Nickie waited. From there, I saw Douglas poking around the lowest of the four levels. Leaning against a low wall, I watched everyone except Nickie descend to the lower levels.

While everyone else was busy exploring the room, Nickie rolled her chair over to me. "Aren't you curious?"

My eyes glanced at the two levels of screens where people used to sit, watching. A large floor to ceiling metal machine blinked and whirred as it encompassed the entirety of the lower level.

"Mazie says that that is an original computer. For decades, computers were so large they filled entire rooms," Nickie said.

"Hey, kids," Dad called. He waved us down to the lower level where he stood with Douglas.

As we reached the bottom of the steps, Exie said, "Nickie, Mazie says you took to this system naturally."

Nickie nodded.

"How would you like to run the Command Center?"

Nickie's eyes opened wide. "Really?"

Smiling, Exie answered, "Really. You'll be in charge of the scopes and communicating with me in the main bunker."

"I can do that," Nickie said. I thought she would burst at any second.

"We're putting two people in each scope right now," said Exie. "Get ready, Sergeant."

Mazie led Exie, Char, and Brayden out of the Command Center. Once they were out of view, Nickie did a little crazy dance before inspecting each station.

"Xavier," Douglas said quietly, "this facility uses a secure frequency. I am going to tweak my surveillance equipment to use this same frequency. My nanobud will work with the system. Only the three of us will know the details of this plan. Get this set up. I'll return shortly."

After Douglas climbed the stairs, I looked at Dad for an explanation.

"You were right," he told me. "It is the only way."

Walking up the steps, Dad asked, "Nickie, where's my station?"

"Right here, Dad," said Nickie, walking to the side on the second level. "I even found you a headset. Xav! You going to stand there or are you going to help?"

Jumping a little, I asked, "Where do you want me?"

"Level three."

"Command," Exie's voice broadcast. "This is scope three."

Nickie ran to the top level. "Scope three is recognized," she said as she sat in her chair.

While Dad did his own thing, I helped Nickie check each scope's master controls. After the eight scopes were manned and checked, Mazie brought Char and Jett into the room.

"Exie wants to keep it all in the family," Mazie said. As she handed us guns, she added, "Jett needs to learn how to use all of this."

Nickie showed Jett each station except Dad's. Char, Jett and I divvied the remaining stations between us. After many checks and rechecks, Mazie brought us dinner.

"Feeling comfortable with the controls?" Nickie asked all of us, although the question was mainly directed at Jett.

"It's not as confusing as I thought it'd be," answered Jett. He smiled at Nickie.

Smiling, she blushed, then quickly looked away.

"Command, this is scope two," a voice said over the loud-speaker. "We have a dot on our radar screen. Approaching from the northwest."

"Can you get a visual scope two?" Nickie asked.

"Working on that now."

"I want scope two's radar on my screen now," Nickie said. She sounded so authoritative.

"Command, scope two again. We see a thin gray line on the horizon. It is coming this way."

"All scopes keep watch on the northwest sky," Nickie said

into the microphone.

"Exie, this is Command. We have a possible drone in sight," continued Nickie. "It's about twenty kilometers out. Be here in less than fifteen."

"Run stealth. Close all doors. Coms dark till it passes," Exie commanded.

Char sealed the door. "Switching to stealth," Nickie said. "Scopes, hatches sealed and coms dark unless new." She flipped a switch that changed all the lighting to a dark orange.

I imaged people in the main bunker running around to close all the many doors while Exie's voice instructed them over the speaker system.

We sat in silence, watching the dot travel across the radar screen. My heart pounded wildly. Its strong beats thumped in my eardrums. My eyes could not peel themselves away from the radar screens as the dot jumped from one screen to another. Nothing moved besides that dot and the sweeping line that detected it.

The dot disappeared from all eight screens. I forgot how to breathe. Nickie raised her hand, telling us to keep still.

After an eternity of breathlessness, Nickie said quietly into the microphone, "All scopes, scan the sky."

We waited with bated breath until we heard, "Scope four is clear."

"Scope one clear."

One by one, each scope reported clear skies.

"Good work, scopes. Keep watching," Nickie said. "Exie, coast is clear."

"You may disengage stealth mode, but stay on high alert,"

said Exie. "Great job, Sergeant."

"Thank you, ma'am," Nickie said with a fleeting smile. Sitting back in her chair, she pushed her light hair out of her face. When she caught Dad's eye, she said, "It has begun, hasn't it?"

"Some would say that it never finished," said Douglas, crossing the bridge. "We don't need to worry about that drone returning. Between here and the rails, someone is going to shoot it down."

"Meaning?" said Char.

"We need to worry about when they come to find who did," Douglas answered. "Everything ready, Caleb?"

"Yes," Dad said. "All we need to do is check it with Xavier."

Douglas approached me. Holding out his hand, a small dot rested in his palm. "Nanobud. It's a two-way radio. With your index finger, place it just inside the outer cartilage of the entrance of your ear canal." As I did as he instructed, he continued, "Easy to insert. Easy to remove. Hard to detect. Say something."

"Like what?" I said.

"Lower your voice to a whisper," Dad said in my ear.

"Wow," I whispered. "It's really clear."

Dad turned a few knobs. "We're good."

"Remove it," Douglas told me.

Placing my finger in my ear, the nanobud easily slid onto the pad of my fingertip.

"You could have been scratching your ear," Jett said.

Over Douglas' shoulder, I saw Mazie cross the bridge.

"Let's call it a night," she said. "Nickie, flip that switch."

I could not see to which switch she pointed.

"Jett, you're staying with us. Exie already brought your things."

"Thank you, Mazie," Jett said.

We followed Mazie through an old corridor to a plain cement wall. She placed her hand on the cement. Green lights over her hand lit before the wall opened. The hidden corridor led us directly to Mazie's bunker.

"Xavier, I hope you don't mind sharing your room with Jett," Mazie said.

"Not at all," I answered. "Come on, I'll show you where it is."

Jett looked around to see nothing but bright colored puffs.

"Your things are already there. You just have to put them away," Mazie added.

Relieved, Jett followed me down the main tunnel to my— our room.

Three large sacks sat in the middle of the floor. I showed Jett where he could put his things and which bed was whose.

"You don't have much stuff," Jett observed.

"Nickie and I left with only what we were wearing." I sat on my bed trying not to watch Jett put his things away.

"That was really brave." Closing a drawer, he said, "So, that's your dad?"

"Yeah."

Emptying the first bag, Jett asked, "How'd you find him?"

"Whitetail," I began.

"I knew it!" he interrupted with a gleam in his eye.

He stuffed the two full sacks and the empty sack under his bed. I must have had a confused expression on my face because he said, "Those are my parents' bags." He sat on the bed facing me. "My mom's family are mercantiles. Her sister and brother-in-law still run the store. My dad had a knack for procuring rare and hard to find items. One day, my parents left to pick up some things for the store. They never returned."

Jett took a deep breath. "They've been gone two years now. Having no siblings, Exie fought for my independence to keep the house out of my aunt's hands. I think Exie suspected my aunt having a hand in my parents' disappearance." Lowering his dark head, he said, "That's why I want to apprentice with Whitetail so badly. I need to find out what happened to them." He paused, then said, "You finding your dad has given me so much hope."

"Knock, knock," said Douglas from the doorway. "Sorry to interrupt guys, but Xavier, it's time."

I nodded knowing full well that I volunteered. That thought did not make following Douglas out of my room any easier.

Chapter 16

He brought me to a small room not much different than Exie's war room. Around the center table, Dad and Mazie studied a map.

As I stood in the front of the map with them, Dad said, "We are here." His finger encircled a large area of the map. Moving his finger northwest, he said, "PC one-five is here." Grabbing a pen, Dad continued, "The main gate is here." He made an x. "Electrical access panels are roughly every fifteen meters." He drew an x at each spot. "Their only protection is from the elements. They'll be much easier to get into than the one in our condo."

I smiled briefly.

"You'll be installing nanonodes," said Douglas. "They bite into the wires, giving us access to their entire electrical system.

After you install the nanonodes, you run like you have never run before. I have weapons stashed here, here, here, and here." He also drew an x on each spot. "Hidey-holes are here, here, here, and here." He depicted those with circles. "If you get stuck out there, we will come and get you. Once in a hiding spot, you do not leave that spot. Each hidey-hole has food, water, blankets, and a first aid kit."

Nodding, I studied the map.

After Douglas made me change into the same clothes I wore when we rescued Dad, the four of us entered the command center. Douglas gave me the nanonodes. I placed the two tiny circles connected by a thin wire into my pocket before securing the nanobud inside my ear.

"I'll be on the other end of the receiver," said Dad. "If you need anything, you let me know."

"'Kay, Dad."

He gave me a hug, trying to tell me that all would be all right. I didn't want to let go, but I knew we had to get Mom. Reluctantly, I let go of Dad, then followed Mazie through the old tunnels.

We did not speak until Mazie stopped in front of a large steel door. "This is as far as I go," she told me. "Once I lock this door behind you, there is no way back." Taking a deep breath, she looked at me with morose filled eyes.

After turning a series of wheels, Mazie pulled open the thick door. The light from the corridor poured into a dark, damp tunnel. Putting a hand on my arm, she breathed, "Good luck, Xavier."

I stepped into the tunnel, leaving Mazie behind. Once my

hand touched the right side of the tunnel, the light faded. With a large boom, I was plunged into darkness. One foot stepped in front of the other. My gloved hand stayed connected with the bumpy wall. A musty stench infiltrated my nostrils. Focusing only on the sound of dripping water, I pretended not to hear the scurrying of tiny feet. In my head, I repeated Douglas' instructions: *follow the right side of the wall.*

When the dripping turned into lapping, I knew my exit was near. The wall ended at a corroded grate, just like Douglas said it would. A gentle push allowed me to escape into the fresh air. I took a good look at the river peacefully lapping the bank onto which I stood. Turning away from the river, I took shelter in a nearby grove of young trees.

"I'm out," I whispered.

"Good," said Dad. "Remember to keep the river in your sight as you walk."

"I am." I pulled the hat over my face, then proceeded slowly. The moon had not yet risen, keeping my path dark.

From a distance, the lights from PC one-five shot into the dark sky. Following the light, the electrified perimeter fence appeared in my view.

"Dad, I can see the fence," I barely whispered from behind a tree.

"Can you see an access panel?" Dad asked.

"No." I walked parallel to the fence. A metal box as tall as I was sat in front of the fence. "I think I found the main grid."

"Even better," I heard Douglas say in the background.

Surveying the area, I said, "No one's watching it."

"They fear no one," Dad said. "But, I'd be surprised if there was no security."

"I'm going to run towards it."

"Be careful."

I took a deep breath. Running from tree to tree, I kept watching for Protector Units, but found none. My stomach churned uneasily. From the protection of the trees, I ran towards the box as fast as my legs could go.

Wild heartbeats pounded in my ears as I studied the box. On the side, an old fashioned padlock kept the box safe. Behind the box, thick plastic coated wires led inside PC one-five.

I picked up a small rock off the ground. The sharp pointed edge cut a slit into the soft plastic wire encasement. I pulled the nanonodes out of my pocket. My gloved hand clumsily tried to push the nanonodes into the slit. Removing a glove, the nanonodes squeezed through the slit. After feeling them chomp onto the wires, I whispered, "Done."

"Now run like your life depends on it," said Douglas.

No one needed to tell me twice. Quickly pulling on my glove, I ran into the trees. I counted fifty paces like Douglas told me to do. As I searched for a hiding place, I said, "In the woods."

"Good," said Dad. "Find a place. Stay there. Douglas will come to get you."

"We're in," I heard Douglas celebrate in the background.

I was closing in on one of Doulgas' hidey-holes when I heard, "No! Come back! No, no, no, no, no."

"What happened?" I asked.

"It stopped transmitting," Dad answered.

My legs slowed. "Automatic override," I muttered. "I can

fix it. I'm going back."

"Xavier," Dad's stern voice reminded me of his reprimands. I could almost see his steely eyes staring at me. "You will not."

Turning around, I said, "There's no other choice. Affixing the nanobud to the nanonodes will circumvent the override system."

"You can get caught," Dad pleaded. We had already risked too much.

I did not want to fail. PC one-five was once again in my view. "Chance I have to take. I'm going in." Running back to the box, I removed my gloves. Lifting the hat off my face, I whispered, "Hope this works. See you all soon." I placed my finger in my ear, then removed the nanobud.

"Hey, you!" a male voice yelled from behind me.

"Been spotted," I whispered into the bud. "Love you, Dad."

As I carefully placed the nanobud into the slit, I could hear my dad yelling, "Xavier! Xavier! Get off me! I have to get my son!" The thick protective plastic covering muffled any sounds coming from the nanobud.

"I'm talking to you," said the voice.

Hearing footsteps, I put my hands on the chain link fence.

"What are you doing?" the voice accused.

Turning my head away from the city's lights, my eyes focused on a kid not much older than I, approaching me in his dark blue Protector Unit uniform. He pointed his laser gun at me.

"I'm lost," I said.

"ID," he said.

"Lost that, too," I said.

"Come with me." As I walked with him, he spoke into his

com, "Base, this is Perimeter Patrol, I found a stray, no tag."

"A stray?" I asked, trying to make small talk.

"Happens more often than you think," he told me. "You're not the first to get lost out here. You won't be the last."

Glancing at my feet, I muttered loudly, "Easy to get lost when everything looks the same."

"Yeah," he agreed. "I hate being out here. Helps to keep the fence in constant view."

I grunted in agreement, but said nothing more. My mind wandered to Dad and Nickie who were worrying about me. As we approached the gate, my focus changed to me. I had been gone for over a week. What was going to happen to me?

Another Protector met us at the gate. When the gate buzzed open, the man said, "Come on, Kid."

I walked through the gate alone. It clanged shut behind me. For the first time when I walked through the gate, I felt imprisoned instead of protected by the fence that surrounded PC one-five. My chest clamped. Breathing labored.

"I'm Thane," said the man who met me. His tone was warm for a Protector. "Let's get you situated."

Thane led me into a small room inside the gate complex. In the room's blinding white light, Thane looked to be around the same age as Dad or Douglas.

From behind the white plastic desk, he said, "Left thumb on the clear plate."

Seeing a two-inch clear rectangle on top of the desk, I placed my thumb as instructed. Within seconds, my ID photo and information popped above the desk.

"I'm going to issue you a new ID card, Xavier," said Thane.

"Have a seat; it's going to take a few minutes to print." He had a fatherly way about him. Missing my dad, I wondered if I was ever going to see him again.

Before I could even look at a chair, two Protectors barged into the room. "Sorry, Thane," one said, "he has to come with us. Orders."

Thane nodded, allowing them to take me away. Before I cleared the doorway, I was sure that I saw a flicker of concern in his eyes.

Chapter 17

With me in the middle, they marched me single file down a long, stark hallway. The narrowness made me long for the wide tunnels of the bunkers. Opening a narrow door, the first Protector stood aside so that I could enter. Shutting the door behind me, they left me in a closet of a room with a small clear plastic table and two matching chairs. I chose the chair facing the door so I could see my visitor enter.

Alone in the holding room, I knew they watched me. Would I show fear? Would I show anxiety? Sadness? Remorse? Somewhere in another part of the complex, my body language, temperature, breathing, and heart rate were being analyzed.

Leaning back in the chair, my legs stretched, hitting the chair across from me. My eyes focused on the plain white door.

When it opened, an older man wearing a highly decorated dark blue Protector Unit uniform entered.

"Bored out of your mind, Mister Kelton?" he asked somewhat amused.

"What do you want, Mister Many Bars?" I asked in return.

Ignoring my out-stretched legs, he sat. His eyes searched me for a sign of weakness. Finally, he said, "What happened?"

"Do men as highly decorated as yourself always interrogate lost teenagers?"

Mister Many Bars leaned forward to place his arms on the table. "You've been missing for over a week. I'd like to know what happened to you."

Sitting up in the chair, I put my elbows on my thighs. My fingers played with my knee as I stared downward. I knew I had to tell the truth—or at least I could not lie. They would know. Taking a deep breath, I stared at my interrogator.

"My sister and I were having one last family picnic. We had gone to see the tree that was planted in our parents' memories. At some point, Nickie said bear. We ran. Our jackets flew into the river. I had no idea where we were."

"Where is your sister?"

My gaze dropped to rest on the table. "Her shirt started choking her. I couldn't get it off." Glancing at him, I said no more.

"Then what?"

"Came across some people who fed me and gave me a place to sleep. Then, I found my way back."

I looked at him and he at me. Without breaking his gaze, he reached inside the jacket of his uniform. His hand emerged holding a dark gray plastic cylinder.

"Care to explain this?" he asked.

"It's a scrollpad."

"It's *your* scrollpad," he rolled it across the table to me.

At my touch, my scrollpad unfurled, laying flat on the table.

"No one, not even our top computer engineers have been able to open or interact with your scrollpad," he said. "How did you manage it?"

Clarity flashed in my mind before I answered, "Advanced biometrics."

"Impressive, Mister Kelton. Can you duplicate it?"

"My mom and dad helped me. Since neither one is here, that would be impossible."

Mister Many Bars looked disappointed. "Out of curiosity, why did you need such advanced security on your scrollpad?"

Shrugging nonchalantly, I said, "Got sick of others copying my homework." I tapped the bottom corner of my scrollpad causing it to roll back into its protective cylindrical shape.

Without another word, Mister Many Bars left me alone with my scrollpad.

Innocently sitting on the table, my scrollpad tempted me to use it. I wanted to check the status of the nanonodes, try to communicate with Dad, or find Mom. But, I knew I could not. They were waiting for me to use it.

I had no friends that I wished to contact. No family, as far as they knew, to notify of my status. To them, I was nothing more than a loner teenager with nothing but a pension for electrical gadgets. Yet, even loners with no lives need reasons. Ignoring my scrollpad, I leaned back on my chair and waited.

When the door opened again, a woman entered. Barely looking at me, she said, "Mister Kelton, come with me and bring your scrollpad."

Chapter 18

I wrapped my fingers around my dormant scrollpad, then followed her into the hall. Almost as tall as I was, she unrolled her scrollpad. The insignia on the screen was familiar. I came across it on some of my dad's old college stuff. A triangle inside a shield shone on her screen. On the shield, solid blue capped vertical red and white stripes—thirteen in all. The triangle had a golden hue slightly darker than the thirteen golden rays that emitted from the shield. Three rays burst on top of the shield and five rays on either side. Along each side of the triangle was one Latin word. Read together, it said, "*Novus ordo seclorum.*" Dad told me once that it translated to *new order of the ages.* When I asked him what that meant, all he said was, "It was taken from Virgil." Asking him about Virgil was fruitless. I had forgotten about finding the insignia. Watching her dark hair bounce slightly as she walked, I wondered where I was being taken to next.

Using her scrollpad, she remotely opened doors through which we walked. The multitude of narrow hallways brought us to an elevator. Her scrollpad controlled that, too. The elevator doors opened to reveal another long, narrow hallway. Halfway down the hall, we stopped in front of a plain white door.

"Your quarters, Mister Kelton," she said. Opening the door with her scrollpad, she continued, "Get some sleep. Someone will come get you in the morning."

Walking into the room, the door slid shut behind me. I faced a large wall of windows. Between me and the windows were a small table and chairs and a small couch. My eyes found a bed off to the side and a kitchenette situated on a small portion of wall in the large, open room.

Fully clothed, I laid on the bed. I opened my scrollpad, then quickly scanned for electrical devices. Finding only household items, I performed a more thorough search. Awhile back, I tweaked my scrollpad to see through walls to find any and all electrical components. After scanning every inch of the room, I found no monitoring devices. To my delight, I discovered a small electrical panel hidden in a wall.

I wondered if they were watching me through the large windows. Turning off the lights with my scrollpad, I waited for my eyes to adjust. I set my scrollpad on the nightstand as I approached the floor to ceiling windows.

Studying the darkness, I pondered my direction. Everywhere my gaze fell was dark. My room faced the wilderness. PC one-five had low-voltage, minimal light polluting lights that ran throughout the night.

While my eyes tried to search the dark wilderness through the window, the only thing I could see clearly was my faint reflection. Light brown hair poked out from underneath my hat. Golden brown eyes stared back at me like they knew something I did not. Blinking, I took one last glance into the darkness. Satisfied, I returned to my scrollpad.

Still draped in darkness, I brought my scrollpad over to the panel. Four small hex screws secured the panel cover to the wall. I tapped my scrollpad. A tiny screwdriver fell into my hand from a hidden compartment. Unscrewing the cover, I smiled to myself. I had always defied the Pod City, well before I had heard of Redux Radix.

I connected my scrollpad to the wires easily. My skeleton key gave me backdoor access to the system. The scrollpad told me that I was in the residence of the research complex outside PC one-five proper. Mom and Dad worked in their respective wings of the research complex. I wondered what they wanted with me, but trying to hack into their encrypted files was a bad idea considering where I was.

Focusing my attention on the Electric Commission's system itself, I found the wiring where I put the nanonodes. They were completely undetectable, like Douglas said. Since I knew where they were, I uploaded system information onto them. I hoped that Douglas could use it. Before succumbing to sleep, I returned the wall and my scrollpad to normal.

I awoke to tapping on my arm. "Mister Kelton," said a young voice.

When I opened my eyes, a smiling face hovered over me.

"Good, you're awake, Mister Kelton," he said. "You need to take your shower and get changed, Mister Kelton. You have a big day ahead of you."

Sitting up, I looked at him. The boy was no older than thirteen or fourteen. His hair sprang like dark ropes out of the top of his head, resting wildly next to his dark skin.

"I'm sorry. Who are you?" I tried to ask as politely as possible.

"I was assigned as your assistant," he chirped. "The name's Gideon. Never been an assistant before. I got your clothes laid out for you and put your badge on your lab coat. Mister Kelton, if you don't get ready soon, you're going to be late."

"Gideon," I said getting out of bed, "please call me Xavier. Mister Kelton is my... was my father."

He nodded as I wandered into the bathroom.

A breakfast of cornflakes in milk made me miss the warm cooked grains of the settlement. Gideon had me don my lab coat and grab my scrollpad before leaving the apartment.

Leading me through the complex, Gideon did not have a scrollpad. He opened doors using his ID badge.

A side door off the corridor opened into a large, bright room. Natural light poured through clear double doors. Behind me, the door we came through said *restricted* on it. Cushioned benches and potted plants filled the space. Gideon and I walked over to a large opening in a wall where a woman greeted us.

"Mister Kelton is reporting for work," Gideon said to her.

She glanced at her scrollpad. "Yes, of course," she said. "I just need to initiate your badge, Mister Kelton."

As I handed her my badge, her badge caught my eye, glimmering in the momentary sunlight peeking over the counter. The words Electric Commission floated over the holographic mark of an original compact light bulb.

"Here you go," she said. "Just swipe on the door at the side."

Taking it from her, I walked over to the door. When I noticed that Gideon was not behind me, I turned my head.

"I'll be here when you get back," he said with a smile.

Feeling a tad uneasy, I swiped my badge.

The door buzzed open. As I walked through, a guy with a lab coat and badge like mine met me in the narrow hallway.

"Xavier Kelton?" he asked.

I nodded.

"Peyton Cumberland," he said. "I'm a first year apprentice, too. Follow me. Says here," he pointed at his scrollpad screen as we walked, "you will be working in Doctor Young's division, Experimental Research. I hear they do some top secret stuff. Not that you will be, mind you. That needs high level security clearance."

"Where do you work?" I asked.

"Product Improvement. It's a good first step to really understanding how things work. In a few years, I will be primed for Research and Development, the non-experimental kind." Peyton led me through a door that opened automatically. "Now, only the top level in the Electric Commission use their scrollpads to open doors because they need both a badge and a secure passcode to enter some areas. As far as we're concerned, our badges will open all doors to which we have access using RDIF chips. Only have to physically swipe to get in. Very convenient." He smiled as though he had thought of it himself.

"Anyway, there is only one junior apprentice and one senior apprentice per department. Your position changes when a higher-up leaves his or her position. Here we are—the Experimental Research Division. I can't enter, but you can. You are to see," he read off his scrollpad, "Patrice. She will upload everything you need onto your scrollpad. See you around the residence, Xavier."

Peyton walked off before I could thank him. I stood in front of an unassuming white door. Taking a step towards it, it opened.

I walked into some sort of waiting room. Benches lined the walls while a lone small table sat near the far wall. A rather round woman entered through a door that I did not see. She kept her eyes on her scrollpad. "You must be the new guy," she said without looking at me. "Follow me."

She led me through the open door.

"You are going to need your scrollpad," she said.

Removing my scrollpad from my pocket, I opened it. After a second, the display said, "Welcome, Xavier. Please take the elevator."

I blinked.

"Follow the instructions on your screen," she said to me. Finally lifting her eyes to look at me, she continued, "Doctor Young is waiting for you, wherever he is."

My eyes searched for an elevator. The screen said, "Three paces forward."

During my third step, a metal door slid open. I entered the elevator. As soon as the door closed, the box dropped quickly.

My stomach lurched so hard that I thought I was in a free fall. When the whir changed to a hum, I knew the elevator was slowing.

The door opened to reveal a dark cavernous room. My scrollpad told me to walk ten paces and meet the man in charge.

After ten paces, a voice said, "We finally meet, Xavier Kelton." Out of the shadows, a small man approached. "I am Doctor William Young," he said. "You are a year earlier than I expected, but I have been ready for you."

"You have been ready for me?"

"To join me in my work," he explained with a warm smile. "I have been keeping tabs on you since you were three years old."

My jaw dropped a little.

"You showed incredible aptitude even then. Of course, when you broke into the secure server at the age of six, I knew you were special."

"Thanks," I said. I did not know what else to say.

"You ask the right question, Xavier—how." Doctor Young began walking through the space.

I followed as he talked.

"Further assurance of my decision came when you arrived just now. Even I couldn't access your scrollpad. Those messages I sent you were mere projections onto your screen." I could hear him smile. "This dark space leads to the experimental chambers. But first, your office."

He led me to a cream colored door. Tapping on the keypad, he said, "Basic door code is eight-one-five. You'll want to change that. As little as three. As many as nine."

The door opened. We entered a small room with a comfortable looking chair behind a cream plastic desk.

"Fully integrated with the latest technology," said Doctor Young. "The wall, floor and ceiling change views. You can be at the beach, in a rainforest, or in the Milky Way. It is as limitless as your imagination. For now, the tour is over. I will leave you to work."

"Doctor Young," I said.

He turned to face me.

"What work am I doing?" I asked.

"Oh, yes. You are to find a cash cow."

"A cash cow?" I did not understand.

"The United States is bordered by four countries—Quebec, Canada, China, and Texas," he explained. "Find out what they want the most. For what things are they willing to pay a lot of Globals? Then, we make it and sell it to them."

"That requires unrestricted access."

"Which we have."

"We do?"

"Xavier, my boy," Doctor Young put a hand on my shoulder, "my department has full autonomy. Pod City laws do not apply to us." A smile flashed across his face before he left me in my new office.

Sitting in my chair, I was not sure if I could trust Doctor Young. He had to answer to someone. I wished I knew to whom.

Chapter 19

My desk had an omniposition keyboard and a scrollpad docking station. Pressing the power button, I let the office boot. Holographic screens asked for setup preferences. I tried many different surrounding scenes. In the ocean was too dark and confining. Middle of a wheat field was too boring. Desert made me thirsty. Glacier made me cold. The noises of a tropical forest drove me crazy. Finally, I chose a view from the Swiss Alps in summer. Standing in my office almost gave me the urge to yodel.

Checking the system, I found that I had unobstructed access to everything. I also found a keystroke logger and half a dozen cameras in my office. All of it watched what I did. Not bothering to change the door security code, I wondered what would happen if I disengaged all the spying devices.

With a wry smile, first I disabled the keystroke logging software. Secondly, I shut down the computer override program. No outside system was going to be able to use mine. Third, with a wave to the camera, I cut those off as well. Finally, I took my trusty screwdriver from my scrollpad. Removing the panel under the desk, I made permanent changes to its motherboard.

Back in my chair, I ran a diagnostic. When I was satisfied that no one could manipulate the office, I changed the entrance code. One number that changed once the door closed was all I needed.

Paranoid, I scanned the cameras around the complex. No one was coming for me. I could not even find Doctor Young. Keeping the camera feed running in the background, my computer made a map of the Doctor's department.

The map continued to grow as I moved it to a side screen. On the main screen, I developed what I called a spyder. It spoofed my computer's source to the internet to originate inside the country where it collected information. The internet that I was used to was highly restricted and filtered. What waited for me to explore was a cyberworld full of people speaking their minds, reports of what the world was really like, and stores with items I've never seen. The spyder was my weapon against getting lost or distracted in a world full of new.

I studied the map as it rendered more detail while my computer scanned the internet. Other offices sat off the main chamber. Further off the main chamber, large rooms had multiple security measures. My imagination did not want to guess their contents. Catching a hallway, my eyes followed it around the secure rooms. At the end of the hallway was a staircase. The map had not rendered enough to show where it led.

A ding reverberated around my office. On the top of my desk, an orange square flashed. The title said, "Inter-Commission Message." Behind the title, a watermark depicted a triangle on a shield.

When I touched the orange square, a small screen popped up in my face. "Join me in my office. —WY," it said. The note did not tell me where his office was. Superimposing the map with the camera footage, I decided that Doctor Young was in the only other office without a camera feed.

I found his office easily. As I approached the door, it opened automatically.

"Come in, Xavier," Doctor Young said with his back to me. He stared at formulas that covered every surface of the office.

The door shut behind me.

"I'm impressed," he said without turning around. "You removed yourself within minutes. Your distrust is founded. *They* shouldn't know what we do. What's that old saying? Oh, yes. You are not paranoid if they really are out to get you." He chuckled. "Not to worry. Socializing in the cafeteria or in the residence isn't problematic. I'd advise you to stay away from the nosey ones. Come see me once you've found something."

The door opened and I took my cue to leave. His words, *your distrust is founded*, echoed in my ears as I returned to my office. Once inside, I performed a security check. Since no one had tried anything, I returned to my work.

I thought that browsing an unrestricted internet would have been more fun. Instead, I found the trivial mundane chatter a waste of time. The details of strangers' lives did not appeal to me. I didn't care who was dating whom, what was bought, where someone went, or what someone had for dinner last night. Perhaps if I knew them, then I wouldn't be so apathetic.

More interestingly, the map expanded beyond Doctor Young's wing. And as the map expanded, so did the camera feeds. Those I studied while my spyder collected information.

The rumblings of my stomach made me notice the time. Believing that I had missed lunch, I browsed the Electric Commission's Employee Handbook. "Lunch is served from 11:00 a.m. to 1:30 p.m. If you know you will miss lunch, or did miss lunch, vending will be available from 10:00 to 10:45 a.m. and from 2:00 to 3:15 p.m." Before closing the handbook, I read about arriving and departing times. "No employee will be admitted any earlier than 7:15 a.m. nor any later than 8:20 a.m. Employees may leave beginning at 4:52 p.m. All employees must vacate by 6:03 p.m."

Each department had its own vending. Ours was up the super fast elevator in a room off the main hall. Taking one look at the vending machine, my stomach stopped grumbling. The machine held nothing more than vitamin water and nutrition bars. I yearned for the ones we had in school that sometimes stocked fruit snacks. Picking a cherry flavored water and a chocolate flavored bar, I sat at one of the two small tables to devour my meager feast.

When I returned to my office, I hastened my escape plan. Map rendering became a higher priority than the spyder. For the rest of the afternoon, I learned about badges and security protocol.

By the time my alarm buzzed to tell me the workday had ended, my head felt like it was going to explode information. My feet retraced their steps to the Electric Commission lobby where Gideon sat waiting for me. He smiled brightly as I approached.

Walking through the residence corridors, Gideon asked me, "Is it exciting?"

"Is what exciting?"

"Working for the Electric Commission," he clarified.

"Oh." I thought about my clandestine work. "It's work," I answered.

Gideon looked disappointed. "I always imagined that working with circuitry would be exciting," he said.

"It can be," I assured him. "But today I mostly stared at screens all day."

As we left the elevator, I asked, "What did you do today?"

"Errands. Things like food and your belongings."

"My belongings?"

Gideon did not have to explain. As soon as the apartment door opened, I saw two large bags on the couch. I barely remembered packing before the picnic. However, I did only remember packing one bag. The other had to be Nickie's.

"I can help you unpack if you'd like," Gideon offered.

Staring at the bags, I threw my lab coat over the back of the couch. With my scrollpad unfurled in my hands, I scanned the room.

"What are you doing?" asked Gideon.

One new device registered on the screen. My eyes found the source—Nickie's bag.

"Mister Kelton?"

I unzipped her bag. Reaching my hand inside, I felt as though I invaded her privacy.

"Xavier?"

My fingers grabbed a cylindrical object. Retrieving it from the depths of the bag, I held her scrollpad in my hand. I set it on the table before falling into a chair.

"Are you okay?" Gideon asked.

Staring at the closed scrollpad, I said, "I miss my sister, Gideon. I miss my mom, my dad." I sighed. "I miss them all."

Gideon looked at me, but I couldn't read his expression. Was it pity? Was it understanding? Was it disgust?

"Food is in the fridge," he said finally. "I'll see you in the morning."

I nodded to let him know that I had heard him.

After he left, I began to heat some food. Using my scrollpad, I darkened the window wall to shut out the evening sun. When the timer beeped, I brought Nickie's scrollpad over to the small dining table with me. I perused her scrollpad while shoveling food into my mouth. Most of the content was school related. Other useless stuff were messages to and from her friends. Exploring further, I found a hidden folder.

I smiled. Inside was poetry. I never knew she wrote poems. One labeled *untitled* caught my eye. I read:

Darkness quakes my heart
Ruthlessly depart
Pieces of my soul
Reveals gaping hole

Mending time will take

Vengeance mine to make

Staring at her words, I could feel the sadness and the anger. I read the lines over and over. Anger morphed into resolve. *Make vengeance.* I had a plan.

Chapter 20

My trusty screwdriver had Nickie's scrollpad in pieces within minutes. After fixing the security holes, I hardwired her scrollpad to mine. I uploaded my paranoia software. It ran unnoticed in the background.

With hers running my software, mine was free to concentrate on something new. My ten o'clock timer beeped. Pausing my project, I hardwired my scrollpad to the system. Someone left a file on the nanonodes. At first glance, the file was empty. Looking deeper, the file relayed a message.

It said, "All of us, young and old, would help Grandma make her rhubarb and raspberry preserves. Making preserves was not just a family function. It was a task good neighbors would help with as well."

Dad's words made me smile. Grandma referred to the white farmhouse where Nickie and I found Mazie. Rhubarb and raspberry meant Redux Radix. Making preserves was Dad's way of letting me know they were planning to get me out of PC one-five. Dad talking about good neighbors helping told me that they were gathering people from other settlements as well.

I pondered the best way to respond. My problem—I was not a wordsmith like my sister. Ones and zeros were my language. But, it was a dead language. People did not care about the order of the ones and zeros anymore. Creating binary code was a computer's function. Thinking I could use the concept, I focused on the letters E, C, D, W, and Y.

I added to the file, "Someone needed the job of tasting every container. Getting fingers in the batches had to be a drudge. Won't you agree?" Reading it over and over, I hoped Dad would understand that I had a job at the Electric Commission with Doctor William Young.

Morning arrived quickly. As I emerged from the bathroom, ready to go, Gideon poured a glass of juice.

"How are you?" he asked, barely glancing at me.

"The best I can be," I answered.

Half smiling, he handed me the glass.

"Aren't you having some, too?" I asked.

"I'm your assistant," he said, looking confused. "I already ate my breakfast."

Digging into a bowl of cereal, I said, "Are you sure you don't want anything?"

He shook his head.

"At least sit down."

Once he sat, I asked, "More errands today?"

"Is there something you need me to get?"

"No," I said as warmly as I could. "I'm just curious."

"School," he said disappointed. "Are you ready?"

Donning my lab coat, I left the apartment with Gideon. He escorted me through the residence. As I learned the route, I had Nickie's scrollpad in my pocket gathering data.

Before Gideon and I parted at the door to the Electric Commission, I said, "Have a good day."

His bright smile returned. "You, too," he said.

Crossing the lobby, I heard my name. When I turned, I saw a group of my peers in lab coats. I recognized a face. "Peyton," I said.

"Without those kid guides, one could get lost in this place," he said.

One by one, we swiped our badges.

"Maybe see you at lunch," Peyton said to me before we disappeared into our different departments.

Descending into the depths of my office, I immediately checked to see what my computer gathered overnight. The map it rendered was great and it kept expanding. My work project, however, needed some clarity.

After tweaking my spyder, it gave me a list of possible projects. Reading minds, predicting crimes, more efficient energy, disease cures, and drought solutions made the list. However, only one thing stuck out as truly project worthy. People wanted a better way to control and interact with their computers and devices. Choosing telekinetic interfaces from the list, I had my spyder search for plans. While my computer worked, I headed to lunch.

The cafeteria was centrally located between the three commissions housed in the research complex. Armed with a plastic tray, I stood in line for my food. The food line eventually spit me out into a jungle of white lab coats. Aimlessly, I navigated, trying to find an empty space.

"Hey! New guy!" a voice called.

I turned to see the face of a guy I saw that morning with Peyton.

"You can sit here," he said.

"Thanks," I said, sitting on an empty attached stool.

"I'm Ridge," he said. "And I forget your name."

"Xavier."

"This place is crazy. Takes some time getting used to," said Ridge. "Learning your way around is half the battle. Have that kid guide of yours give you the full tour. And take notes. The kids can only give you one."

"Really?"

"Yeah. Found that out the hard way. The guides only stick around for a week tops."

"Good to know, Ridge, thanks," I said. "So, what do you do here?"

He ate a few bites before saying, "Electrical Maintenance. I sit and watch a screen all day. Birds and rodents give me such headaches." Shaking his head, Ridge laughed heartily. After chugging his drink, he said, "After your tour, Xavier, come to the rec room. We'll all be there. Anyway, I got to go. Hope to see you later."

"Sounds good. Bye," I said with a smile. After he left, I

took my time finishing my lunch. I wanted to give my computer time to complete its work.

Back in my office, I looked at the multiple failed attempts at telekinetic interfaces. The products that helped our minds directly interact with electronics varied. From glorified voice recognition software to computerized contact lenses, no one could get it quite right. Second skin gloves looked promising, but they short-circuited and shocked their users. Brain implants had an "unfavorable mortality rate." With all the failed plans before me, I pondered how I would do what all those scientists could not.

The contact lenses showed the most promise. Their flaw was limitation of movement. The eye could not convey enough information to do exactly what the user wanted. Or the contact lens could not detect it.

My idea was a biometric headband that reached from temple to temple. I did not know if it would work, but it was different from everything before me.

After compiling a presentation, I headed to Doctor Young's office. I raised my knuckles to knock on his door, but it opened before they made contact.

"Come in, Xavier," he said. Doctor Young sat at his desk, typing. His office walls still were filled with formulas. Looking up at me, he said, "What did you find?"

"Telekinetic interfaces."

"Interesting. Do you think it will work?"

"Yes," I answered. "My concept will read the electrical pulses of the brain."

"How?"

"Through a person's temples."

Doctor Young's eyebrows scrunched briefly as he looked at me. "Put together a presentation of past attempts. Then, outline how yours will be different and what kinds of technologies will be needed to do this."

"I already have."

He smiled at me. Rising from his chair, he said, "Come."

Doctor Young led me through the underground lair. Finally stopping to open a door, we walked into a room four times the size of my office.

"Load your presentation onto this server," he instructed.

I wondered if he knew that I was not using my scrollpad as I transferred a copy of my presentation to the room. Within seconds, everything I gathered popped into the center of the room. Doctor Young encircled the holographic screens. He pushed the failed plans to the sides so that my plans for the headband hovered alone in the center of the room.

After studying it, he said, "This is new thinking. Very impressive, Xavier. We could sell both the plans and the prototype if manufacturing is problematic."

"What is the next step, Doctor?" I asked.

"Consultations with a molecular biologist, a sub-atomic scientist, and a neuroscientist," he answered. "All three people will look at the plans, then give their recommendations about what is needed from them to make it happen. No one will know who the others are. Their reports will be in this room in a couple of days. Your job is to check periodically. Your badge will open this door. See you tomorrow, Xavier."

When I returned to my office, I noticed that my map was

rendering much more quickly. Before my alarm signaled that it was time to leave, I had it find all electrical components in and around PC one-five.

In the lobby, Gideon greeted me again. As we strolled through the residence I asked, "How was school?"

Gideon shrugged.

"That bad?" I asked.

"Didn't learn anything new," he complained. "Same old reading and math."

"But reading and math are important," I said.

"I already have a job," said Gideon. "I don't want to go to school anymore."

"What will you do when you are no longer a guide?" I asked him.

We entered the apartment as he explained, "Guides usually work for the Sanitation Commission when they grow up. *I* am not a guide. I am your assistant. Permanent job."

Hanging my lab coat, I asked, "Why do I have an assistant while others do not?"

He stared at me, then said, "When you're someone like me and you're handed a future, you don't ask questions. You take it."

I sat on the couch with my scrollpads while Gideon stayed in the kitchen area. Nickie's scrollpad began compiling all the data it had collected.

"Gideon," I began, confused, "what do you mean someone like you?"

He finished what he was doing then sat on the couch, facing me. "They often call us Zetas. Most people have no idea we exist. We are kept away from people like you."

"Why?"

My concern must have shown because he smiled before explaining further. "Zetas are the children of prisoners and workers in the labor camps. We have our own school and our own dormitory."

Labor camps were full of people who were either released from their time in prison or did a lesser crime. "I don't understand," I said. "Why are children punished for their parents' crimes?"

His dark brown eyes looked directly into my light brown ones. "My mom," his voice was low, "went to prison while she was pregnant with me. And that's where I was born."

"Why did she go to prison?"

He shook his head. "She never told me."

"And your dad?"

"My mom always said that my dad was taken from us just before she landed in there." Gideon gazed at the floor as if it were interesting. "I used to visit her everyday in her cell," he said without taking his eyes off the floor. "Then, one day, I went to visit her and she wasn't there. I asked where she was." He closed his eyes. "They told me that she died." His fingers wrapped around his shirt.

After wiping his eyes with his sleeve, he said, "I'm an orphan. Just like you."

My heart went out to him. I wasn't an orphan anymore, but I couldn't let him know that. "How long ago did she die?"

"Three years."

"I'm so sorry, Gideon," I said.

He gently nodded his head.

The oven buzzer beeped. Gideon jumped off the couch, then hurried to the kitchen.

Frozen on the couch, I did not know how to clear the sad awkwardness. I followed Gideon to the kitchen where he stirred something before putting it back in the oven. "I'm sorry if I made you uncomfortable or divulge something you didn't want to," I said.

"It's okay," he said. "You seem to understand. Usually those who aren't Zetas don't."

Gideon left me to eat dinner alone. I munched while checking my project on my scrollpad. Stage one had completed.

After hardwiring the scrollpads, I transferred my creation to Nickie's scrollpad. Affectionately, I called it the V-bomb. Once on Nickie's scrollpad, I commanded my V-bomb to multiply.

Making sure Nickie's scrollpad was set on transmit but not receive, I left the apartment to spend the evening wandering the halls of the residence. As I passed a device with which the scrollpad could interact, like another scrollpad, a camera, or a door opener, Nickie's scrollpad deposited a V-bomb onto the passing device. Each of those devices, in turn, would deposit a V-bomb onto every new device with which it interacted. The V-bomb would creep onto every interactive device within PC one-five and beyond in a matter of days.

To reach as many hosts as possible, I made my way to the rec room. Only half the lights were lit in the large rectangular room, casting a soft dim glow. A group sat in an oval, looking at their scrollpads.

"Hey, Xavier," Ridge called. "Glad you made it! We're

playing poker. Deal you into the next round?"

"Maybe next time, Ridge," I said.

Ridge nodded happily before returning his attention to his scrollpad.

For a moment, I felt badly having to infect his scrollpad. But, then it passed as I meandered to the far end of the room. From a lone seat, I watched my peers play games on their scrollpads, ignorant of my V-bomb, which would infect every device they met.

"We don't bite, you know," said a soft feminine voice.

When I found the source of the voice, my eyes swam in pools of blue.

"I'm Talise," she said as she pulled over a chair.

Her blue eyes contrasted beautifully with her tan skin.

"I hear you're Xavier," Talise continued. She almost purred when she spoke.

"Yeah, I am," I said. I felt extremely stupid, and I was sure my cheeks flushed.

Laughing a little, she smiled, then quickly looked down.

Knowing I should say something, nothing came to mind.

Thankfully, Talise asked, "Where are you from?"

"Here."

"Really?" she said with her eyebrows raised. "I'm from PC six-three. A few months ago, I came to work for the Nanotechnology Commission. The rest of my family works in either the Water or Farming Commissions. Since you're from here, maybe you can show me around PC one-five sometime. Meet your family?" Talise smiled sweetly as her pool blue eyes gazed intently into mine.

"No," I found my mouth saying.

"What?" She blinked. I swore her inviting blue eyes turned to ice.

"My family isn't with me anymore," I explained. "There's a memorial tree."

Her gaze softened as she leaned towards me. Placing a hand on my knee, she said, "I'm so sorry, Xavier."

"Thanks," I said, trying to lean back, but my back was already pushed against the chair.

"I have to go," said Talise. She slowly lifted her hand from my knee, completely sliding her hand across it. "It was nice meeting you," she purred. Her hand severed contact, but she did not drop her gaze. "By the way," she whispered, "I'm in room three eighty-five."

My eyes could not stop watching her saunter away from me. When she glanced over her shoulder at me, cold crawled through my body. The group of girls she joined giggled. I wished I had spent more time with Kai. Knowing that I was going to see Kai again, I returned to my apartment several floors above the rec room.

In my pajamas, I hardwired my scrollpad to the system. Expecting another story, the nanonodes were my first stop. The blank file held encryption. I recognized my dad's encrypting—a method he taught me a long time ago.

"Xavier," it said, "it is best we are direct with each other. I'm assuming they put you up in the residence. I met the good doctor years ago. He's relatively harmless, just a tad eccentric and completely obsessed with his work. They won't let you outside the gates for a while. Bake your ID badge in a medium oven for fifteen minutes. That way, it will still open doors, but it cannot collect data on you. Remember all that I have told you. Love, Dad."

Racking my brain, I tried to remember. Nanolife. Sigma Epsilon Delta. Every Pod City is connected via electrical wires. The Electric Commission is the most powerful commission. They run the Central System in what used to be Washington, D.C., now known as Capital City. Capital City is the only Pod City without a number. The Central System controls the national power grid and is rumored to hold a massive database.

I knew what Dad wanted me to do. Quickly I responded, "Dad, I have an upper floor view of the countryside from my apartment in the residence. Don't worry about me. A heat wave is coming. I have fond memories. X."

Stage two I called Heat Wave. It was a simple computer program that caused machines to run a little faster and a little hotter than they should. Unlike my V-bomb, Heat Wave had to be manually uploaded to a specific device.

Luckily for me, I could do it all from my scrollpad. I uploaded Heat Wave onto the central transformer, the section transformers, and the light system of PC one-five. After a couple of hours, Heat Wave had been uploaded in each Pod City.

I switched my focus to Capital City. Uploading Heat Wave was easy. I put it in multiple places of the Central System in case of overrides and failsafes.

The screen of my scrollpad flashed red. Security sweeps had started. I had to disconnect before they found me. Without shutting down my scrollpad, I pulled the wires apart. Blue and white sparks flashed and my nose caught a whiff of melted plastic.

Hasty knocking rattled my door.

After pushing the wires into the wall, I screwed the panel back on.

"Xavier, it's Gideon," Gideon said in hushed tones that accompanied the knocking. "Can you let me in?"

"Be right there," I said.

I picked up my scrollpad. It had paid the ultimate price. Walking towards the door, I placed my dark scrollpad gently on the table.

When I opened the door, Gideon fell into the apartment. His dark face was streaked with wetness. He looked at me with red, puffy eyes.

"What's wrong?" I asked.

"I've done a bad thing," he said.

My heart skipped a beat.

"Don't blame you if you don't forgive me," he said. "But, I'm here to make it right."

"What did you do?" I asked.

His hands fidgeted with his shirt as he looked at the floor. "I lied to you," he said. "I'm sorry."

"What did you lie about?" I asked. My voice sounded stern like my dad's when he would get disappointed in me.

Gideon dropped onto the couch, then put his face in his hands. Through his hands, he said, "I'm supposed to be spying on you."

"Supposed to?"

He lifted his head out of his hands. "Yeah. I haven't been telling them everything. Like how you have two scrollpads."

"And?"

"I can't do it anymore," he said.

My rising anger slipped a few notches. "Why not?"

Gideon took a deep breath. "They told me that you needed to be watched. That you were suspicious. But, then I found someone."

"Who?"

"Your mother."

I collapsed onto the couch. "Where? Is she all right?"

"She's in prison," he said. "She's strong. A friend of mine works there. As we walked past the cells, I happened to mention to my friend that I was your assistant. Your mother must have overheard because she called out to me from behind the bars on the door."

"What did she say?"

"She was glad that you were doing well. She mourned for Nickie." Gideon paused. "She... she told me things."

"What things?" I wished he would spit it all out.

"Things that made me remember," he answered. He looked out the window. "Made me remember what my mom told me the day before she," he mouthed the final word, "died.

"I'm named after my dad. He's Gideon, too. Before I was born, they took him from us. My mom never exactly told me why. All I know is that he was trying to give us a better life and he was exiled to the labor camps. My mom said that it was an injustice, so she tried to free him. Doing so, she ended up in jail."

His dark eyes looked at me. "Your mother said that my parents did nothing wrong. They were wrongly punished. There is nothing wrong with wanting something more for your family than what you have. She said that there is nothing wrong with wanting to be free, to live a life on your own terms and make your own decisions."

Gideon paused again. "That day my mom said good-bye to me, she said that she probably wouldn't see me again. My mom didn't die in jail. She was taken and," he closed his eyes, "executed."

Tears gushed down his face. His breathing got weird.

I did not know what to do. I felt as though I intruded on his sorrow.

After he wiped his eyes and blew his nose, Gideon said, "Your mother said that I have done nothing wrong. They were in the wrong. They lied to you. I can't spy on you anymore."

I felt betrayed, yet sorry for Gideon. He was only toeing the line after all. "Why come to me now, in the middle of the night?" I asked.

"I had to. My badge is in my room. I didn't want them knowing I came to see you. A friend of mine let me through the doors." He answered with his big brown eyes brimming with tears that looked as if they could overflow without warning. "I will understand if you want a new assistant."

"I don't want a new assistant," I said. "I want an assistant I can trust."

"You can trust me."

"Then, help my mom escape."

His eyes widened. "I don't know how," he said softly.

"Go back to her now. Tell her I said that Nickie found Grandma's white farmhouse to be amazing and that a heat wave is coming with a vengeance. You are to obtain whatever she needs."

Gideon nodded.

"I will see you in the morning. You are to tell no one about this," I instructed. "And, do not let them know that you stopped spying on me."

Nodding more, Gideon ran out of the apartment.

I could feel the burden of hope on his shoulders as I examined my scrollpad. The wires were scorched. Some of it could be bypassed, but other parts needed replacing. Deciding to tackle it in the morning, I tried to get some sleep.

Chapter 21

After a rough night of waking every half hour thinking they were coming for me, the shower tried to wash the sleepiness down the drain. Gideon entered the apartment as I tried to force my scrollpad to roll into its dormant shape.

"What happened?" asked Gideon.

"I was stupid," I answered. Abandoning it, I asked, "How'd it go?"

"You're having a hot breakfast this morning," he said with a sly grin. Gideon turned the oven on to medium. While both of our ID badges cooked, we ate cereal and laughed in a sleep-deprived stupor.

"Your mother asked for a bucket full of stuff," Gideon told me. "I'm collecting everything today. Is there anything you need?"

Glancing at my dead scrollpad, I said, "Flex wire and any other parts that can be spared."

Gideon and I parted at the usual door. As my badge opened various doors, I wondered how Mom and Dad knew about baking the badges.

In the dark experimental wing, Doctor Young called to me. He looked more disturbed than usual. "Mister Ambers has requested to see you," he said.

"Who is Mister Ambers?"

"He is the Commandant of PC one-five and Chieftain of the Northern District," Doctor Young explained.

"Why does he want to see me?"

"I do not know, but I am supposed to take you to him. Come with me."

Doctor Young's sad demeanor led me through the dark cavern. I did not know if I should have been scared or flattered. All I knew was Nickie's scrollpad still worked. It sat benign in my pocket while depositing V-bombs on every device it met.

We walked through the corridor that passed the secure rooms. The corridor ended with two sets of doors. The first set opened, revealing an elevator. As I followed Doctor Young into the elevator, I noticed a sign depicting stairs next to the second set.

I held onto the rail behind me as the elevator jolted us upwards. When the doors finally opened, we stepped into a room full of pod car tracks. Doctor Young led me into a nearby pod car. He swiped his ID, then entered our destination.

The pod car lurched around a circular track. Soon after

choosing the path, we emerged into sunlight. I had been inside for so long, I had forgotten how bright day could be. Out of the three hundred sixty degree pod car windows, I squinted at PC one-five. We zipped away from the city below us. Trees masked our destination.

Beyond the trees was a barbed wire chain link fence. A gate slid open as the pod car approached. The pod car crept around a circular track, giving me a chance to gawk at a large window and cement structure. Single levels jutted out from the building here and there. I wanted to push them back in to make a tidy rectangle.

Doctor Young sighed when the pod car finally stopped. Before the pod car door opened, I noticed Protector Units patrolling the area. They paid no attention to us while we walked to the large door.

The door opened as soon as Doctor Young pressed his thumb on the pad. I followed him into a large, sun filled open area. The pink floor looked to be marble. Colored rugs with intricate designs artfully covered parts of the floor. The furniture had a flair with which I was unfamiliar. As we climbed a short flight of stairs, the overall look both impressed and intimated me.

"Gentlemen," said an oily voice, "come in; come in."

We both cautiously entered an open office. The man to whom the oily voice belonged sat in a large richly colored chair behind an equally large wooden desk.

"Don't look so forlorn, William," he said. "I'm not stealing him from you. I simply wish to welcome the young Mister Kelton."

Doctor Young's body relaxed. "Mister Ambers, Xavier Kelton as requested," he said.

"Thank you," Mister Ambers said. "Why don't you wait downstairs, William."

Nodding, Doctor Young then left me alone with Mister Ambers.

"Sit down, Xavier," he said.

I sat on a smooth brown chair in front of his desk. The window behind Mister Ambers overlooked a large well-manicured garden.

"What do you think of my house, Xavier?" he asked.

"It is very nice, Mister Ambers," I said in disbelief that he lived in it.

He smiled. "Thank you," he said. "I've worked very hard to acquire all these things. Ancient rugs from Arabia and India. Handcrafted furnishings from China. African artifacts and European antiques pilfered during the revolution."

Ironically, all the things Mister Ambers surrounded himself with were so full of detail while he was relatively nondescript. He yammered about his possessions and I still had no idea why I was summoned.

"Tell me, Xavier," he said, "how would you like to have a house separate from the Pod City filled with things of your own and a private pod car?"

"That sounds very nice. But, I don't understand," I said.

Mister Ambers leaned forward. "I am handing you an opportunity. The same opportunity I offered your father, by the way. You can earn Globals and spend them in the world market. You would be included in the higher social order. When you have children, they will attend the best schools."

"Earn Globals," I repeated.

"Yes," Mister Ambers said eagerly. "From your inventions. You would receive a generous percentage. What do you say?"

From the way he looked at me I could tell that he wanted an answer right then. "Would I still work for Doctor Young?" I asked him.

"Of course," Mister Ambers said.

After my dad refused Mister Ambers, he was imprisoned. I could not count on Whitetail to save me from execution. And since I had not finished my plan, my decision was made for me. "I would like that very much," I said to Mister Ambers.

"Wise decision," he said with a smile. "I'll have your assistant prepare everything. You'll move into your new house this evening. Now, get working on that headband."

"Thank you, Mister Ambers," I said, taking my cue to leave.

As I walked towards the steps, Mister Ambers called me back. I stood in front of his desk while he said, "If you can figure out how to make those headbands work both ways, there will be a generous bonus for you."

"Both ways?"

"Yes. But, that can come later," he answered. "Just something to think about."

Downstairs, I returned to Doctor Young.

While we rode back to the Electric Commission, Doctor Young said, "Welcome to the fraternity."

"The fraternity?" I asked.

"Sigma Epsilon Delta."

Chapter 22

Joining Sigma Epsilon Delta was inevitable. After all, I was my father's son. I wondered if they would have extended an invitation to Nickie at some point.

Getting off the elevator, Doctor Young said, "Since you are officially one of us, there is something I want to show you."

His eyes sparkled, but I did not like the way he said *one of us*. No, it was not the way he said it. It was the fact that he said it. *One of us*. Those three words filled me with disgust. To someone like Peyton Cumberland it would be a badge of honor. I, however, felt dirty. Contaminated, not privileged. As I followed Doctor Young into an extremely secure room, I pondered if they thought or hoped I was going to let my guard down because they included me.

The first door opened automatically. Doctor Young used a

passcode from his scrollpad to open a second door. When we came to a third door, he entered a nine digit code onto a keypad then placed his hand on the pad to be scanned. A light flashed green. The thick third door peeled away. We entered a small plain room.

"Watch the screen," Doctor Young said. When he flipped a switch, the room darkened.

A screen that encompassed half the wall turned white. On the screen were gray something-or-others. They moved quickly.

"What is that?" I almost whispered.

Elation showed on Doctor Young's face. "Nanolife," he said. "Technically, they are in the lab next door. This screen connects to a nanoscope."

"Wow. What do they do?"

"*They* are the future of energy," Doctor Young explained. "Imagine never having to recharge the power cell in your scrollpad. Never having to worry about the wind or the water flow powering the turbines. Or pollen and dirt on the solar panels, especially on a cloudy day. With never-ending self-replenishing energy, we will never have to burn fossil fuels or use harmful chemicals in batteries."

"How does it work?" I asked.

"I knew this would interest you, Xavier. Life, as we have always known it, is carbon based. Nanolife, on the other hand, is aluminum based. Aluminum, besides conducting electricity well, is lightweight, malleable and ductile. Plus, it naturally resists corrosion." Doctor Young looked like a proud father.

"How does metal live?"

He chuckled. "Nanolife is not really alive like you or I.

They do not have the capacity to reproduce. Aluminum's superconductivity allows it, with my secret process, to be an energy source."

"Interesting," I said. "Do we use it yet?"

"No, no. Nanolife has yet to leave this lab," Doctor Young answered. "I am still doing long term testing and simulations. Then, I will have to find a way to produce it on a large scale."

My eyes followed the movement across the screen. "What about," I began slowly, "it reacting with other objects?"

"Nothing to worry about," said Doctor Young. "It will be contained in inert heatproof cases. So, it will resemble a battery pack." He flipped the switch that returned the room's lights.

As we left the lab, I knew that Doctor William Young was completely ignorant of the horrors of his creation.

Sitting alone in my office, my sleep-deprived mind rewound the morning. Mister Ambers wanted telekinetic interface head-bands that worked both ways. My original concept was to have thoughts control computers. Going the other way meant that computers controlled thoughts.

If I had not already been sitting, I would have fallen to the floor. How could I have been so stupid, so blind? I did not consider repercussive uses. Our minds, our thoughts, were the only bastions of privacy we had left. If that were taken away, what would we be?

Interrupting my self-flagrant thoughts, my alarm told me to go to lunch. I made sure Nickie's scrollpad still transmitted V-bombs before I left my office. My plan needed to continue.

In the cafeteria, I slithered slowly around the tables under the guise of searching for an empty seat. My food became lukewarm by the time I found a seat near the food line. I didn't care about my food. Every scrollpad inside the cafeteria had been infected with a V-bomb.

After lunch, I visited the room where my headband project came to life on the holographic screens. No one had written an analysis. I left the room, hoping that my V-bomb would destroy all copies of the plans. Not wanting to return to my office, I wandered the corridors.

Beside most doors, the signs said, "Lab," with a number under it. Eventually, the labs gave way to project rooms. All of which were also numbered. In the midst of the project rooms a sign said, "Scrap Room." Curious, I entered.

On my face, a wide smile grew. I could have constructed a whole new scrollpad and then some with all the stuff loaded on the shelves. Searching the shelves, I filled my pockets with everything I thought I could use.

When I returned to my office, I dumped the spare parts on my desk. Some things I snatched so it looked like I was working on the headband. Everything else I tucked into my clothes. I did not want to be seen removing items from the Electric Commission. Such things were not allowed.

Gideon met me at the Electric Commission door. Small talk passed the time as we walked through the residence. Inside the apartment, Gideon had already placed bags on the bed for packing.

"We have an hour," Gideon said. "A Protector will come for us and escort us to the new place."

"Have you been there yet?" I asked.

"No. I signed for a food and a furniture package," he said

while folding my clothes. "I, too, had to pack." He threw me a wry smile letting me know he had smuggled items into his bag.

I layered my clothes with the spare parts and my dead scroll-pad.

Between the two of us, we had four bags. One was Gideon's. One was Nickie's. Two belonged to me. Somehow, I gained an extra bag of stuff since I returned.

When the door buzzed, we each took two bags. I let Gideon exit first while I made sure the door shut behind me.

"This way, Mister Kelton," said the Protector.

I stared at the back of his head while he led Gideon and me out secure doors. Outside the back of the residence sat a rover. I stopped, almost dropping my bags.

"Pod cars don't reach this door," the Protector said. He smiled at me.

I thought I recognized him.

He took our bags. Putting them into the back of the rover, he said, "We met briefly. The name's Thane. I'm stationed at your house for your protection."

Thane did not elaborate. As I jumped into the rover, I wondered from whom or what he was protecting me.

We traveled on a dirt and gravel path I did not know. A large, rover-sized gate opened for us. Thane drove us outside the electrified fence into a treed section. The bumpy road took us past houses amongst the trees. Finally, we turned off the road, driving over paved pod car tracks.

The rover stopped in front of a two-story building. "Here it is, your new house," said Thane.

"The whole thing?" Gideon asked with his face pressed to the rover window.

Thane chuckled. Getting out of the rover, he said, "The fence is rudimentary, but it will work."

I stared at the few wires running from pole to pole, which semi-enclosed the property. From the back of the rover, we collected our bags. At the front door, Thane punched the security code on the keypad.

"You can change it once you're settled," said Thane.

The door swung open. I stepped into an open great room not unlike my parents' condo. The only differences were the opened-back steps along one wall and the lack of large windows.

"Bedrooms are upstairs," said Thane. "Why don't you two unpack. I will start dinner." He looked at me warmly as Gideon and I carried the bags upstairs.

I took the master bedroom. As I carefully unpacked, Gideon picked a bedroom for himself. Removing the clothes, I left all the electronic components in my bag.

We met Thane near the kitchen. "Dinner won't be ready for a few more minutes," he told us. "Come with me."

Thane led us out the backdoor. We stood in the middle of the tree enclosed backyard when he whipped out a laser gun. I took a step backward.

"You have nothing to fear from a gun," Thane said.

Not unless one is pointed at you, I thought.

"I had a chance to inspect the property," continued Thane. "The fence may not keep bears out. If you come face to face with one, or any undesirable creature, both of you should not hesitate to shoot."

Gideon glanced at me with raised eyebrows.

"Come here, Xavier," said Thane. "Laser guns are set to close range stun by default." He thrust the gun into my hands. "Next on the dial is long range stun. Last is kill. We are going to practice with long range stun. Adjust your dial."

I turned the recessed dial until it clicked.

"Bears and the like will most likely run away if hit with this setting," explained Thane. "If not," he nodded his head to mean shoot to kill. "Take your aim at that tree over there, Xavier." Thane pointed to a point beyond the fence.

With the gun in my hand, I aimed at the tree.

"Good. Now, pull the trigger."

My finger squeezed gently. I thought nothing happened. Then, I saw a mark on the tree.

"Very good, Xavier," said Thane. "You are a natural." He laughed. "Don't look so shocked. It's all hand-eye coordination. And practice. Gideon, your turn."

Gideon looked petrified, yet excited. Thane took a different approach with Gideon. Softness exuded from Thane. Once Gideon took his shot almost missing the tree, Thane led us back inside.

"We'll practice more tomorrow," Thane told us.

"You're coming back?" I asked.

Thane scooped food onto three plates. "They really tell people nothing," he muttered. "My quarters are over the garage," he said in a more pleasant tone.

Gideon and I brought our plates to the table.

"The powers that be wanted to protect their investment," Thane explained during dinner.

I understood *powers that be* to mean Mister Ambers and *in-*

vestment to mean me.

"I volunteered for this job," Thane added.

"Did you know it was me?" I asked, laying off the pretense.

"Yes. That is why I volunteered." Thane took a few bites of his food before saying, "You and your sister were placed on a watch list. Commander Gregory does not interview people lost in the wilderness."

"Commander Gregory is the guy with all the bars?" I interrupted as I pictured Mister Many Bars.

Nodding, Thane continued, "I don't know what they want from you, Xavier. But, if they had it already, you'd be in jail or elsewhere."

Immediately, I thought of my scrollpad. They wanted the technology. And, they wanted a mind-controlling headband.

"Guess I'm useful," I said.

"For now," Thane added darkly.

We finished dinner in silence. I was not sure how much I could trust Thane. After the dishes were clean, I returned to my bedroom to fix my scrollpad.

I dumped spare parts that both Gideon and I collected onto the bed. Methodically, I removed and replaced what I had destroyed in my haste. Finding newer and better parts, I replaced perfectly good parts, too. Once I replaced the side panel, I rebooted.

My scrollpad ran faster and smoother. The extra zettabyte I added gave me so much more storage space. All the leftover components I stuffed into an empty bag. With my improved scrollpad, I thoroughly scanned the house.

Walking from room to room, I found no listening devices, no

watching devices and no monitoring devices of any kind. Only one thing in the house interested me—the access panel in my bedroom closet.

I barely reached the closet door when someone knocked softly on the bedroom door.

"Xavier," said Gideon, "can I come in?"

"Of course."

Entering the room, Gideon closed the door behind him. "I'm going tomorrow. Anything?" he asked.

"Talk about here," I said. I wanted Mom to know that I was now living in a perimeter house. "Also," I chose my words carefully, "aluminum. What do I do?"

Gideon looked confused, but he nodded anyway. "See you in the morning," he said.

After he left, I quickly had wires hanging out of the closet wall. I attached my scrollpad, then reworked the doors to open with our badges. When I searched the nanonode, another encrypted message waited for me.

"We will be ready when you are. Be careful. Love, Dad."

I replied, "I moved to a house that Mr. A offered me. I'll be careful. Mom is looking after me from afar, for now. Hope to see everyone soon. X."

Disconnecting from the wall, I brought my scrollpad to the bed with me. I activated the countdown clock. "One more day to go," I said to myself before falling asleep.

Chapter 23

The smell of breakfast cooking lured me downstairs. In the kitchen, Thane flipped pancakes. Gideon stood to the side, watching intently.

"Morning, Xavier," greeted Thane. "You kids need a heartier breakfast than cornflakes."

Not arguing, I took a plateful of pancakes to the table.

"I want to give you another shooting lesson before you leave this morning," Thane said, joining us at the table.

"Do you have to?" asked Gideon.

Syrup dripped from Thane's fork as he said, "Absolutely." After eating another bite, he continued, "We're beyond the borders of the Pod City now. When you first start living on the edges, survival is essential. And, it's not always pretty."

Outside, wind shook the branches. "Moving targets," said

Thane. "I took the liberty of getting each of you a gun."

Gideon looked horrified while Thane pressed guns into our hands. I, however, was glad to learn.

Watching Gideon's hands tremble around his gun, Thane said, "Your father did not fear guns."

His hands stopped trembling as his head raised to look at Thane towering over him. "You knew my father?" Gideon asked.

"I did indeed," nodded Thane. "He was a brave man."

Gideon's small chest puffed out as he took a deep breath.

We took turns hitting various targets assigned by Thane. When target practice finished, Thane said, "You're improving with each shot. If the rain holds off, we'll practice some more later."

As we entered the house, Gideon looked pleased with himself. I pulled him aside while I put on my lab coat.

"Take this with you," I said, thrusting Nickie's scrollpad at him. "You won't be able to open it. Just carry it wherever you go."

Taking the gray cylinder from me, he asked, "What if someone asks?"

"You're transporting it for me."

Nodding, Gideon stuck it in his pocket.

Thane escorted us to the pod car. "I'm placing both guns in the storage bin, in case you need it," he said. "Bring them into the house with you when you come home."

Once Thane left us alone in the pod car, I entered our destination. The garage door opened. Looking out the window, Gideon wowed softly as we descended to PC one-five.

My stomach turned over. I had no idea what I was going to do once I got there. Working on the headband was not an option. Stage three of my plan could not commence until my countdown clock reached zero. Waiting was not my strong suit.

Our pod car entered a space in the large pod car garage. Housing only a half dozen pod cars, I did not understand why the garage had to be so large.

Gideon and I entered separate doors. His took him into PC one-five while mine took me into the depths of the Electric Commission with Doctor William Young.

The elevator ride was lonely, but I was getting used to that. It gave me time to think. I wondered if Gideon would come with us when Mom and I disappeared into the wilderness. And when we went, would Thane stop us?

Thane was odd for any Protector I ever encountered. He had some semblance of a soul. So many in the Protector Units mechanically went about their jobs. It was as if they did not really care. Clock in; clock out; get to keep the roof over your head and food in your stomach.

We were always told to do our part in society. All of us were cogs in the machine—working together for our collective survival. Money was the root of all the evils in the world. Money caused the environmental melt down that led to our destruction. Money created the "plague" that killed millions. So, when they created the New Era twenty years ago, money was eradicated from our system. The lack of money brought us a renewal.

Yet, I was offered money—a decent amount of Globals—to do what *they* wanted. If money was as evil as they said, then why was it good for some but not for others? In school, we were taught that social status, which happened to be determined by money, was gone. That stuff was part of the old era. In the New Era, everyone was equal and everything was fair.

The New Era only replaced one social order for another social order. A social order where those with privileges were hand picked by the ruling elite. A social order where Gideon was less than. What kept everybody equal was ignorance of the system.

By the time the elevator doors opened, I regretted eating such a hearty breakfast. The long walk to my office did not help my stomach any.

As soon as the office door closed behind me, an orange inter-commission memo flashed on my desk. Tapping it, a message from Doctor Young opened.

"Let me know when you hear something," it said.

I sat at my desk without having the faintest idea about what he meant.

A second orange square flashed. When I opened it, I read, "From the College of Science and Technology."

Immediately following, a third message said, "I applied for you."

Sitting back in my chair, I sighed. Attending college was the furthest thing from my mind. Those were the thoughts of the old me. Before they stole Mom and Dad from us. Before their plan to break Nickie's spirit and turn her into someone I would not recognize. I, however, would have spent a week or two in boot camp before landing in this office.

Perhaps, I would have been grateful to get out of a year or two of Protector Unit duty. Perhaps, I would have done what they asked without a second thought. Perhaps, I would have been different. Or, perhaps not.

Ignoring the Doctor's memos, I brought the map of PC one-five forward. My eyes found the jail near the perimeter. Outside of that, closer to the river, were the labor camps. Further from the river were the edge houses.

The one with the most electrical components had to have been Mister Ambers' house. Unfortunately, I could not pick out mine. However, they all seemed to back into the woods. Essentially, I could just jump the fence and run.

The map did not show anything further. Pushing it into the background, I pulled up all the files on the desk. One by one, I deleted everything I had done. My web surfing history—gone. My spyder—gone. And, so were the plans for the headband. The only thing I kept was my V-bomb.

I spent the rest of the morning studying the map. My eyes were tiring when my computer dinged. An email appeared on my secondary screen. Opening it, I read, "Dear Mister Kelton, I am pleased to inform you that you have been accepted into the College of Science and Technology. In our rigorous work-study program, you will be able to earn your doctorate within three years."

I merely glanced at the start dates and other stuff about which I did not care. Remembering the three orange memos, I trekked to Doctor Young's office.

"So?" Doctor Young said with eagerness in his eyes as he opened the door for me.

"I'm in," I said, trying to muster a smile.

"And the three year plan?"

"Yes."

"Fantastic," he said.

"How can I get my doctorate in three years?" I asked. "It took my parents much longer."

"As it did me," Doctor Young explained. "But today, higher education is streamlined. Plus, being here gives you... certain privileges." He smiled at me. "Well, I don't want to keep you from telling all your friends at lunch. Congratulations, Xavier."

"Thank you," I said before leaving his office.

In the cafeteria, I sat alone, blending into the white lab coat jungle. Lunch was a necessary annoyance. More than once, I considered setting the V-bomb off early just for my personal amusement. Imagining the pandemonium made me smile.

"What are you smiling about?" asked Peyton as he and Ridge joined me at the table.

Gazing at Peyton's permanently smug expression, I answered, "I just got accepted to the College of Science and Technology."

Peyton said nothing.

"Congrats, man," said Ridge. He looked truly happy for me. "Which program?"

"Three year doctorate."

Ridge's eyebrows raised. "Wow," he said. "Good for you."

Still, Peyton said nothing. Though his food seemed to be the victim of merciless stabbing.

"Thanks," I said with a wider smile than I should have had. Grabbing my tray, I said, "I need to get back. Have a good one!"

Ridge said, "Bye," while Peyton continued his silence.

I left the cafeteria satisfied that lunch was not a total waste. When I returned to my office, I deleted the map.

The rest of the afternoon consisted of scrubbing the hard drives. Scrubbing removed all traces and ghosts of deleted files from the computer. What remained were only the original computer programs and the V-bomb.

When the workday ended, I walked to the elevator, knowing that I would only return for one specific reason. And that reason depended on what Gideon had discovered.

Gideon was waiting for me as I stepped out of the elevator. Walking towards the pod car, I noticed he carried a bag. I dared not ask him what was in it. Even though the skies no longer had ears, the walls certainly did.

I told Gideon all about the College of Science and Technology in the pod car ride away from PC one-five. We even laughed over Peyton's jealousy.

Per Thane's instructions, I made sure the guns accompanied us inside the house. While Gideon ran upstairs with his bag, I draped my lab coat on a hook near the door. In the kitchen, Thane was cooking again.

Sitting on the couch, I checked my scrollpad. The hours were winding down. Gideon placed a small bottle on the coffee table before joining me on the couch.

"Hydrochloric acid," he said quietly. "Combined with aluminum, it makes hydrogen gas."

"Are you sure?" I said, staring at the bottle full of clear liquid.

"Very," nodded Gideon. "And it comes with a warning. Hydrochloric acid will eat through just about anything. Hydrogen gas is highly combustible. It could react with anything in the atmosphere. If it does burn, you won't see the flames without special light."

"Thanks, Gideon. Everything else okay?"

"Yeah."

"Gideon," called Thane as he approached us, "could you set the table please?"

Nodding, Gideon left me alone with Thane.

"I don't know what you're planning," said Thane in a low voice. "And I don't want to know the details. Whatever it is, I am not going to stop you. Just know that they have killed for less." He looked at me so intensely, it was as if he wanted me to read his mind. "We'll practice shooting some more after dinner. Come, let's eat."

The three of us sat around the table eating in silence. Taking a chance, I spoke.

"After shooting practice, can I have my sister's scrollpad?" I asked Gideon.

His dark brown eyes got bigger. "Can't," he said.

"Why?"

"I had to give it to someone," he mumbled.

"Who?" I needed to know where it was.

Gideon's glance shifted from me to Thane, then back to me.

"It's okay," I assured him. "Tell me."

"Your mom," breathed Gideon.

All anxiety I had about the scrollpad melted.

"Sadie's alive?" Thane said more to himself than to either of us.

I stared at Thane. "Who are you?" I demanded.

Slowly, Thane looked at me. "Your only friend."

Chapter 24

He rose from the table with an odd look on his face.

"Where are you going?" I asked Thane.

"There is something I need to do," Thane said.

"What about shooting practice?" Gideon asked.

He looked at us warmly, then said, "You two are great. Do what you need to do. Perhaps we'll see each other again."

"You're leaving?" Gideon asked in disbelief.

Thane gave us a smile before he hurried out the door.

"Where'd he go?" Gideon asked in a panic. "He can't leave us. Not out here. All alone."

"He wouldn't have left us if he didn't think we could manage without him," I reassured.

Nodding, Gideon looked slightly less panicked.

As we cleaned up the kitchen from dinner, I asked, "Are you

coming with us?"

Gideon almost dropped a plate. "Out... out there?"

"What's left for you here?"

If the counter had not been behind him, Gideon would have slumped to the floor. He glanced around the house before saying, "I'm scared."

"The unknown is always scary," I said. I had no idea where that jewel of wisdom came from, but it calmed Gideon. "I need to get ready to go."

"Where are you going?"

"Back to the Electric Commission."

"I'm coming with you," said Gideon.

"Thought you would," I said with a smile. Halfway up the stairs, I stopped. "We may not come back here," I told him.

He breathed deeply before nodding.

In my room, I changed into Dad's thermal image blocking clothes. I took the bag with the spare parts, then headed down-stairs. Making sure my scrollpad was safely tucked in my pocket, I ripped my ID badge off the lab coat. In the kitchen, I searched the cupboards for food. I stuffed my bag with all that I could find.

"I'm ready," said Gideon from behind me.

Zipping my bag closed, I said, "So am I." After grabbing the bottle from the coffee table, I picked up a gun on my way towards the garage door. "Grab your gun and badge," I told him.

With our bags in tow, I led Gideon to the pod car. The gun sat in my lap as we traveled down the hill to PC one-five. I kept the clear bottle in my hand. Gideon seemed calm in the glow of the setting sun.

The pod car came to a stop in a garage parking space. I slid the gun under my shirt then motioned for Gideon to do the same. Getting out of the pod car, Gideon followed me closely. The elevator door opened as my badge drew near.

Together, we stepped onto the elevator. Gideon grabbed the back rail as the box plunged. The bottle was still tightly in my grasp when the doors opened. I motioned for Gideon to be silent as we entered the dark hallway.

Though the hallways looked deserted, I was not sure if Doctor Young had left. I walked as softly as I could just in case. Gideon mimicked me.

When we came to the spare parts room, I stopped. "Get as much as you can," I whispered. Handing him my bag, I let him inside the room.

Alone in the hallway, my empty hand clasped the handle of the gun under my shirt. I could feel my heart beat through the gun.

Finally, the door to the nanolife lab stood in front of me. Taking a step towards it, the first door opened. The second would not open so easily.

Leaving my gun under my shirt, I extracted my trusty screwdriver. Within seconds, I had the access panel beside the door open. After carefully placing the bottle on the floor, I hardwired my scrollpad. The passcode was easily cracked. When the door opened, I disconnected my scrollpad, then picked up the bottle.

I began unscrewing the keypad next to the third door when I heard a door open. A drum pounded in my ears. I slid the screwdriver into my pocket.

My hand reached under my shirt for the gun. Turning to face the intruder, I pointed the gun at Doctor Young.

"Xavier," he said much too calmly for someone with a gun pointed in his face, "what are you doing?"

"The right thing," I said. I showed him the bottle.

Glancing at the bottle his eyes widened briefly. "Science is always the right thing," he said nervously.

I laughed. "So, all those attacks on innocent people are justified because science is always right?" I asked. "My sister being attacked by her shirt was the right thing? I don't think so. Did you know the clothing is embedded with nanolife?"

Genuine shock flashed across his face.

"That nanolife, which you insisted is not really alive, began to reproduce." I was beginning to sound maniacal. "Your nanolife is evolving, Doctor Young. As they evolve, they wage war against us."

Shock turned into sadness.

"Let me into the lab," I demanded.

He shook his head, saying, "I cannot let you destroy my life's work."

"How many more have to die?" My voice cracked with frustration. "I can hack the code and stun you for your hand print."

Doctor Young stared at me.

"You know I can. The choice is yours, Doctor," I said, waving the gun at him.

His eyes fixated on the bottle in my hand. "What is it?" he asked.

"Hydrochloric acid."

Slowly, he nodded. Doctor William Young stepped towards the keypad.

"Know that I was betrayed. I never would have tampered with Caleb's work," he told me.

His fingers touched the numbers. His hand pressed against the dark keypad. The door opened. He turned to face me. Doctor Young was calm as if he had made some sort of peace.

"I enjoyed watching you. You have great potential," he said. "The answer is one. Now, give me the bottle."

"Doctor Young?"

He held out his hand. "The bottle, Xavier," he repeated.

My hand twitched.

"This place is full of combustible gases," he said.

I understood. Lowering the gun, I placed the bottle in his open hand.

"The elevator takes one minute," said Doctor Young as he walked into the viewing room, closing the door behind him.

I ran as fast as I could through the halls. Gideon emerged from the scrap room with full bags. Grabbing my bag from him, I said, "Hurry."

We raced to the elevator. My eyes glanced at the stairs. On a snap decision, I stepped into the elevator.

The doors closed as the box began to push us upwards. Gideon held his side. All I could do was say, "Come on, come on," over and over under my breath.

When the elevator began to slow, I knew we were almost there. It gave me no comfort. I could not shake a sick feeling in my stomach. And I only wished I could blame it on breakfast.

"Do you hear that?" asked Gideon.

A groan echoed in the elevator shaft. The lights flickered.

"What's going on?" Gideon said.

We heard a screeching noise. Orange emergency lights replaced the regular light as the elevator came to a shaking halt.

I looked at the countdown clock. "We still have time," I muttered.

Gideon looked over my arm. "What happens when that reaches zero?" he asked me.

Ignoring his question, I said, "The emergency system has been activated." I thought about the flammable nature of hydrogen gas. "Fire."

"Can you make this go?"

"I can override the system, but for how long?" I looked up. "Escape panels."

With my foot on the railing, I pushed open the panel on the ceiling.

"Climb up," I told Gideon while I extended a hand.

He put a foot on my leg and climbed out of the elevator box.

Throwing an arm towards me, he said, "Grab my hand."

I used the rail to push myself higher so I could grab Gideon's arm. With his help, I climbed on top of the elevator box.

The elevator shaft had dim orange emergency lights every so often. They illuminated a ladder along the wall. We began to climb. I felt as if I were back in the bunker, climbing to the surface.

Another groan echoed up the elevator shaft.

At the top, I found a lever. Pulling it, the door to the pod car garage opened.

I helped Gideon out of the shaft. We ran back to the pod

car.

The pod car climbed the hill more slowly than I would have liked. From the safety of the pod car, I watched a plume of smoke rise from the garage. Sirens rang through PC one-five.

Gideon leaned back in his seat. I could not take time to relax. My muscles ached from the climb. My heart still raced. My pocket vibrated.

I pulled my vibrating scrollpad out of my pocket. The display showed the countdown with less than five minutes.

"Hold onto something. I'm opening the door," I told Gideon.

When I pulled the override handle, the sirens grew louder in the woosh of the wind. I moved to the seat next to the emergency brake. Watching the countdown, I waited.

With one minute left, I put my hand on the handle of the emergency brake. Gideon watched intently. I breathed the numbers as it counted down. "Five, four, three," I squeezed, "two, one, zero." I pulled the brake.

The pod car stopped mid climb.

As the lights blew in the Pod City below us, I crawled out of the pod car.

Gideon followed me outside. "What's going on?" he asked.

"Stage three," I answered.

Sparks burst against the darkening sky like a symphony of fireworks.

Chapter 25

My scrollpad rested in my hand. With a tap on the screen, I initiated the V-bombs.

"What did that do?" asked Gideon.

"Two things. First, it wipes everything clean. Second, it puts me in control," I said. Breathing in the cool evening air, I asked, "Where did my mom say to meet her?"

"She said something about fighting fire with fire," answered Gideon.

Why did my parents have to be so cryptic? I had no idea what that meant.

The loud bang of a gunshot reverberated in the trees. We could not stay on our perch.

I tried to keep the city in view as we ran for the relative shelter of the trees. Stooping near a tree, I surveyed the area. Lights flashed in the city as more sirens wailed.

My scrollpad screen flickered. I had control.

Through video surveillance, I watched people tap and shake their scrollpads. Pod cars stopped on their tracks. Unfortunately, innocent people had to find refuge from the sparks of malfunctioning electronics. Fires spontaneously ignited.

A loud boom rumbled in the surrounding hills. I paged through the surveillance searching for its source. Near the prison, a cloud of dark smoke blanketed the camera's lens. There had to be only one explanation.

"I found my mom," I whispered to Gideon. "Come on."

Gideon started rooting around in his bag. "Wait, your mom gave us something special to wear," he said.

"I am wearing something special. Now, let's go."

He quickly pulled dark material out of his bag. When he put it on, it looked like a sleeveless shirt. Holding a wad of dark towards me, he said, "Please wear it. I don't want to disappoint your mom."

Since he said it like that, I too pulled the dark sleeveless shirt over my head.

We made sure our bags were securely on our backs, then we ran down the hill towards the jail.

The wooded hill was dark. Our run slowed to a brisk walk. Losing sight of the city, I wasn't sure if we were headed the right way.

A crunching noise in front of us caused us to stop. I pulled out my gun, ready to shoot.

A glimmer of blonde hair shone through the darkness.

"Xavier." A voice I thought I'd never hear again quietly

called to me. "Put the gun away."

I saw a tall, thin blonde haired woman walking towards me. A sleeveless shirt covered her clothes as well. Lowering my gun, I said, "Mom?"

She ran to me and scooped me into her arms like only a mother could. Immediately, I felt comforted and safe. All was right with the world.

Mom then smiled at Gideon. She looked worn and tired but determined.

"How'd you find us?" I asked.

She held up a small gray cylinder. "Nickie's scrollpad," she said. "Manipulating the biometrics, it led me straight to your scrollpad."

"What's the plan?" I asked Mom.

"We're freeing the people in the labor camp first," Mom said.

Mom looked at my screen as I scrolled through the camera feeds of the labor camp.

"I'm going to set off a bomb by the fence. Gideon will cover me. You are going to open all the gates simultaneously," Mom instructed.

Gideon and I followed Mom to the labor camp. Hiding in the bushes, Mom said, "Let me know when you're ready."

On my scrollpad, I switched from camera view to override mode. After pinpointing the labor camp, I found the main gate and the labor gates.

"Ready," I said.

"Guns out boys," said Mom. "Do not hesitate to shoot."

Both Gideon and I set our guns to long-range stun. Mom crept out of our hiding place. Reaching the fence, it looked as if

Mom was pouring stuff on the ground.

As wisps of smoke began to rise into the air, Mom ran towards us.

Gideon fired his gun. A man on a perch dropped out of sight.

I opened the labor gates, then disengaged the alarm system.

Mom returned as a boom vibrated my eardrums. With a tap of my finger, the main gate opened.

"Give me your gun," she said, "and lock the Protectors inside."

Without hesitation, Mom fired twice, relieving Protectors of perch duty.

I stared at her.

"Lock!" she said to me.

Finding the Protector Unit bunks, I locked the doors. Only a few escaped.

Mom scooted closer to me. "There should be a weapon cache somewhere," she said.

Using the cameras, I located a room full of guns.

"Great. Lock the inner door, but unlock the outer door," Mom instructed. After I pressed the screen, she said, "At least they can arm themselves. Let's move."

Mom led Gideon and me through the trees. The flickering lights from PC one-five gave the illusion that we were walking through a strobe light filled forest.

"Sadie, wait," called a voice from the trees.

Mom stopped. In the blinking light, Thane approached us.

"Thane?" said Mom.

"Figured you'd come this way," Thane said. "The explosion

at the jail could only have been you." He handed belts to each of us. Mom's had a gun attached. "You'll need these."

"Laser guns with portable rechargers?" said Mom. "They'll know you helped us."

Thane shook his head. "It doesn't matter," he said looking at me. "I couldn't save my son, Sadie. Let me help save yours."

Mom handed me back my gun so she could take the belt from Thane. "Are you coming with us?" she asked.

"I'm on a solo mission, Sadie," he said. "What I should have done a long time ago."

"Eliza wouldn't want—," Mom started.

"Yes she would. Eliza fought then when I could not," he said. "Well, I'm fighting now. I think she'd say, 'Better late than never, Thane.'"

After staring at Thane for a second, Mom slowly nodded. "Be careful, Thane."

He cracked a small one-sided smile. "See you around, Sadie."

Thane disappeared as suddenly as he appeared in the blinking forest.

While we traversed the woods carefully, I asked, "Mom? Who's Eliza? How do you know Thane? And where did you learn how to use a gun?"

Mom stopped. Turning towards me, she smiled nostalgically. "Eliza was my best friend. We grew up down the street from each other. When her parents disappeared, she moved in with us. It was like having a sister. We terrorized the city streets together. Since my father, your grandfather, was a pediatrician, he was one of the first to see the sickness in the small children.

He and my mother made the decision to send Eliza and me away. We were sent to the middle of nowhere, at least as far as we city girls were concerned. That is where we met Thane. His parents were kind enough to take us. Thane's parents taught the three of us how to shoot and how to survive.

"My parents always kept in touch whether is was a phone call or an email. They never told us the entire story. They tried to spare us from the atrocities that were really happening. The last time I heard from my parents was when I got my acceptance letter for the graduate program." Mom closed her eyes for a moment. "They never knew about me becoming a doctor, my research, your father, or you guys.

"While I was busy in academia, Eliza married Thane. Because of Thane's weaponry skills, he was plucked from the population for the Protector Units. When the New Era began, he rose quickly through the ranks. Eliza both married first and had a child first.

"They named their son George after her missing father. George, however, was born with a handicap, which manifested later. Around the age of two, he spent a fair amount of time in the hospital. By the time he was three, the Health Commission decided that George was too much of a strain on the system. He was denied further care. To make matters worse, they recommended that both Thane and Eliza be sterilized."

"What does that mean?" Gideon asked.

"So they could no longer have children," explained Mom. "Thane and Eliza filed an appeal. Then, while Thane was away for special training, their appeal was rejected. Along with a rejection came... a termination date... for George."

Gideon gasped. I felt sick.

"Eliza went crazy. She stormed—unarmed—into the Health Commission. They killed her where she stood in cold blood." A tear streamed down Mom's face. "When Thane returned home, he had to bury both his son and his wife. They then stripped him of his ranks. None of us were the same after that."

After taking a deep breath, Mom said, "Come on. We need to get to the rendezvous."

Mom kept her gun drawn as we walked. The woods were filled with noises that echoed off the hills and the river. Walking silently did not matter.

A laser hit a tree beside me. "That was a warning shot," said a Protector using a megaphone.

We stopped. A Protector Unit stood up the hill from us.

"Citizens," the Protector continued, "you are in violation of Pod City code five-eight-two-one-b, wandering in an unauthorized area, and of Pod City code two-four-six-six-f, illegal possession of firearms. Surrender your weapons and come with us or you will be stunned."

Mom pulled Gideon and me behind her. "Be ready to run," she whispered.

The Protector holding the megaphone dropped to the ground. None of us fired our guns. More lasers shot from behind us.

Mom pushed us into the trees.

A horde of dirty people wearing rags ran up the hill. Armed, they shot at the Protector Unit.

"Run," Mom told us.

The three of us wove through trees. Bodies fell around us,

but we did not take the time to shoot. The trees ended at the pod car tracks that led to the outside houses. We followed Mom across the pavement, running in the direction of the old-fashioned gunshots.

Pavement gave way to grass. Beyond the grass was a treed sanctuary. Half way to the trees, we were bathed in light.

"I must say, I am disappointed in you, Xavier," said a magnified voice. The nondescript oily voice could only have belonged to Mister Ambers.

Ignoring him and the lights, we kept running.

"Guess you are your father's son," he said.

A beam of green light flashed in front of me.

Gideon fell to the ground with a thud.

"Gideon!" I screamed.

He did not move.

I felt something bubble deep inside me.

A Protector Unit began to surround us.

Mom started shooting. "Save yourself, Xavier, I'll hold them," she said.

I looked at Gideon's lifeless form sprawled in the grass. No. I was not losing both my friend and my mom. Whatever was bubbling inside burst.

Seeing nothing but Protector uniforms, I shot at each dark blue coat. Dark blue fell into the green grass. Jumping over bodies, I hunted for Mister Ambers.

Behind the sea of Protectors stood Mister Ambers. Changing the gun's setting from stun to kill, I took aim.

Approaching him carefully, I noticed the contraption he wore. He looked as if he had spokes shooting out of his back.

In his hand, he caressed a small, flat, gray box with a smooth screen.

"Are you going to kill me, Xavier?" he taunted. "Make everything right for everyone who's dead and will soon be dead?"

A pounding reached my ears. My finger pressed the trigger.

He laughed as a sphere of shimmering green surrounded him.

His laugh never reached my ears. Once the green dissipated, I shot at him again. The green shimmered again, mocking me.

"Personal force field," he said. "Absorbs the power of the laser gun." He smiled luridly.

I hated his smile. I hated him. I hated his personal force field. Pure hatred caused me to press the trigger a third time.

Through the shimmering green orb, I saw him position the gray box in his hand. He smiled wider, then said, "With a touch of my finger, I can redirect all the absorbed energy into a single beam."

"You killed Gideon with that green beam," I said.

"I knew you would appreciate the technology. Ready to meet your father, Xavier?" Mister Ambers asked me.

I had no defense against him and there was nowhere to run or hide. I held my breath, waiting for the green beam to hit me.

A gunshot rang in my ears. Mister Ambers collapsed, grasping his side.

"You were always short sided, Richard," Dad said, approaching. "Force fields do nothing against an old-fashioned lead bullet."

Wincing in pain, Mister Ambers looked surprised.

Dad kept his gun pointed at Mister Ambers. "Disappointed that I'm not dead, Richard?" Dad asked him.

"I've always hated you, Caleb," Mister Ambers grumbled. "Caleb, with all the talent. Me, with nothing, as father always reminded." He coughed. "Got his in the end just like you will." His blood covered hands fumbled for the small gray box.

"Not so fast, Ambers," said a deep voice from behind me. "I owe you."

Mister Ambers' eyes found a tall, dark man wearing rags, directing a laser gun at him.

"Masters," breathed Mister Ambers. "Guess I should have listened to Gregory. Be quick."

Masters stretched a large hand towards Dad. "May I?" he asked.

Dad handed Masters his gun without hesitation.

Masters shot Mister Ambers in the leg.

Mister Ambers wailed in pain.

"That was for my wife," Masters said. Shooting him in the arm, Masters said over Mister Ambers moans, "That was for my child." He waved the gun around slowly like he was looking for the next painful spot. "Be quick, you say? I've spent the last thirteen years planning on how I would make you suffer like I have suffered."

Mister Ambers' breathing labored.

"Your pain cannot compare to the pain I've been living with," Masters said. "Perhaps it is best just to take from you, what you took from me." Masters glanced at Dad.

Dad put his arm around my shoulders. Turning me away from Mister Ambers, Dad said, "Come on, Xavier."

As we walked towards Mom, I heard a final gun shot.

"Thanks, Dad," I said.

He squeezed my shoulder.

"Kelton," called Masters as he caught up to us. He handed Dad back his gun, less a few bullets.

In the flood lighted grass, Mom crouched next to Gideon's body. A terrible knot clutched my stomach. I didn't want to approach, but I had to. It was all my fault.

I stood next to Mom, putting a hand on her shoulder. Looking down, it was like Gideon was staring right at me. Then, he smiled. Blinking, I shook my head.

"Xavier," he said.

"Gideon? Gideon," I smiled. "Oh, wow."

"I hurt everywhere," said Gideon, wincing. "I thought these were laser proof vests."

"They are," said Dad. "Designed them myself."

"You were hit really hard, Gideon," Mom told him. "Don't move on your own. We'll help you."

"I got him," said Masters.

Standing, Mom locked eyes with Dad. When they embraced, I looked away to give them some privacy.

The group of people wearing rags joined us. Another man helped Masters with Gideon.

With one arm around Mom, Dad's head motioned for everyone to follow him.

Chapter 26

The reclaimed woodlands gobbled our group as Dad led us to an unknown destination. PC one-five's remaining light faded quickly. Nestled beyond the woods, a tent city bustled with life. Dancing flames of oil lanterns greeted us.

Dad spoke to a man I did not know. Then, he turned to the group. "Those in need of medical attention, come with me. Everyone else, please go with Hunter," said Dad, pointing to the man with whom he had just spoke.

Most followed Hunter. I stayed with Mom and Dad.

When we entered an expansive beige tent, Dad said to a nurse, "We've got a boy who needs to see Doctor Meltac."

The nurse glanced at Gideon, then said, "I'll show you to the empty bed over here."

Gideon's helpers took him to one of the small beds. He grimaced as they helped him onto the bed.

Elsewhere in the tent, nurses attended to patients with a variety of ailments. After making sure that we were fine, Dad ushered Mom and me out of the tent. "You can come back and check on him later," Dad told me.

I nodded. Noticing that Masters stayed with Gideon, I left the tent with Mom and Dad.

Inside another tent, people were talking around a central table.

"Mommy!" Nickie cried.

They ran to each other. I wasn't sure which one cried more or held tighter.

"Oh, Nickie. They told me that I had lost you," sobbed Mom.

After a long hug, both Mom and Nickie wiped their eyes. The four of us joined the table. Dad introduced Mom to Mazie, Douglas, Char, Brayden, and Exie.

"Got to hand it to you, Xavier," said Douglas. "That was some show. Word has been pouring in from around the country. All the Pod Cities are weakened. The Redux Radix is stronger than ever." He gave me a rare smile.

His smile quickly faded when a woman ran into the tent. "General," she said, "Protector Units are boarding the train."

"They're fleeing?" said Brayden in disbelief.

"No. They're abandoning the Pod Cities," Exie said. "Reinforcements for Capital City."

"If they're doing it here, they're doing it from all of them," added Douglas.

"Thank you, Sergeant," said Exie. "If that is all, you may go."

The woman saluted before leaving.

"We need to stop them from getting to Capital City," said Exie, "or our factions there will be destroyed."

"Blow up the rails," Douglas suggested.

"What we need is an electromagnetic pulse," said Brayden.

I pulled my scrollpad out of my pocket. "I can stop all the trains," I said. "I just need to get in range."

Douglas eyed the scrollpad then glanced at Dad. When Dad gave him a nod, Douglas said, "Just Xavier and I go in dark."

"Wait," said Mom, opening Nickie's scrollpad. "We need a way to stay in touch."

Extracting my hidden screwdriver, I opened both scrollpads. "I can modify the scrollpads to be able to send and receive low frequency radio waves. It's old school, but we get more distance," I said while making adjustments.

After replacing the covers, Douglas asked, "Ready?"

I gave Nickie custody of my bag. Checking my pockets for the gloves, I said, "Yep."

Douglas led me out of the tent, saying, "Been camped out here for days, planning and waiting. That laser gun you have might get detected. We'll trade it out for a non-electric version."

We came to a tent with armed men surrounding it. They let us enter without hesitation. Inside, piles of unmarked crates were neatly organized.

"Jett," called Douglas. "Need an exchange."

Jett appeared from behind stacks of crates. Smiling at me, he said, "Glad to see you made it back. What do you need?"

Removing my recharge holster and gun, I said, "A replacement."

"Is that laser?" Jett said with wide eyes.

I nodded.

"Can I?" he asked.

"Sure," I said. "Watch the settings. My mom is with Nickie. She can answer any questions you may have."

Looking excited, Jett handed me a new gun with a holster. "Fires eight rounds. And here's an extra magazine," he said.

"Thanks."

After securing the new gun to my body, Douglas led me outside.

"We're running silent again," he told me as he pulled on his gloves. "Let me know when you are in range."

Nodding, I, too, put on my gloves.

Once we reached the edge of the camp, both of us stretched our hats over our faces. With a thumbs up, we took the first step towards PC one-five.

My heart pounded loudly with each step. A blanket of clouds smothered any moon or starlight. Heavy wetness filled my nostrils. The sky desperately wanted to make my life more difficult and wet.

Flashes of light gave the cloud blanket definite shapes. A little later, booms of thunder rolled above the wilderness. Douglas pointed at the sky, then pulsed five fingers twice indicating that the storm was ten kilometers away.

Reaching the trees, I knew that we were getting close to the Pod City. They liked to pretend that the forest regained control of the land we squandered many years prior. The wind howled a warning—the worst had not yet begun.

The howling masked the sound of our footsteps. PC one-five shone past the trees like a broken beacon. We were getting too close for my comfort, but not close enough for my scrollpad.

A low growl underscored the howling wind. Douglas grabbed my arm. We stopped.

"Do. Not. Move," whispered Douglas.

Motionless, we watched a huge black shape approach. On all fours, it was almost as tall as Douglas and I. I could hear the bear sniff us from afar, wondering if we'd make a good meal.

"When I shoot," Douglas continued, "you will run. Do what you need to do. Then, get back to camp."

"What about you?" I asked.

"Leave me," he ordered.

"I—"

"The shot will bring them. Best if we part."

Before I could argue, the bear rose onto his hind legs. Looming over us, he roared.

Douglas' shot echoed off the low clouds. He pushed me away.

I ran. A second shot rang through the trees.

PC one-five kept getting closer. It was a magnet that did not want me to escape its clutches.

When I could no longer discern my legs, I stopped. Voices carried through the heavy night air. Crouching, I tried to listen.

"Everyone who is not dead or injured," I heard a voice say. "Are the weapon caches cleared?"

Peeking around the tree, I saw the train station. Protectors loaded heavy plastic boxes onto the cargo car.

I was close enough. Hiding behind a tree, I opened my scrollpad. The magnet rail system master control found my screen. With a tap of my finger, I disabled the train engines. The Transportation Commission centralized their entire operation. Everything could easily be shut down all at once and just as easily turned back on. I needed to do more.

My fingers locked the control rooms and the engine compartments. Then, I shut off the power to the magnets that made the trains move. To make sure they could not be turned back on, I diverted the electricity to the back-up system. It would not take long for the excess power to short circuit. My final act was shutting off the power to every car on each train in the country.

Once the lights went out behind me, I knew no one was going in or out of the Pod Cities. With my work done, I retraced my steps through the wilderness.

The crisp sound of gunshots found my ears. I fought the urge to find them. Mixing with the shots was the low, gentle hum of a rover.

"Whitetail will find a way," I muttered to myself. I needed that to be true. Faith in believing he was still alive gave me strength to reach the camp.

Walking past the lantern lighted tents, I peeled the hat off my face. Somehow, I found the command tent.

As I entered, everyone stared at me. "It's done," I told them.

"Where's Douglas?" asked Mazie.

I bit my lip before saying, "Out there somewhere."

Exhaling, Mazie closed her eyes.

Char put a hand on Mazie's arm. "He'll come back, Mazie. He always does."

Mazie simply nodded.

Mom smiled at me. "It has been a long day," she said. "Why don't you check on Gideon?"

"Okay."

Walking to the medical tent, I needed a distraction... or a chair... better yet, a bed. If I could have gone to sleep, then I would have awakened and the nightmare could have been over.

Gideon waved to me as soon as I entered the tent. Before I reached Gideon's bed, I heard my name being called. Turning, I saw dark brown hair and bright blue eyes approaching me.

"Kai," I said with a tired smile.

Smiling, Kai threw her arms around me. "Xavier, I'm so glad you're back," she said.

My arms didn't know what to do at first. They gently touched her back. I had wished that I had removed my gloves so that I could feel her hair under my hands. Before letting go, I relished in her warmth and comfort.

After the hug, I found myself getting lost in her eyes. I would have been happy to stand there with her for an eternity.

"How are you doing?" asked Kai.

"I'm not sure yet," I said. Coming back to reality, I continued, "Want to meet a friend?"

Her eyes somehow became brighter. "Sure," she smiled.

Together, we walked to Gideon's side.

"Kai, meet Gideon," I said.

"Hi," Kai said to him.

Gideon had a stupid smile on his face. His lips barely eked out a, "Hi," in return.

"How are you feeling?" I asked Gideon.

"Okay," he said. "Got some cracked ribs. Doctor wrapped them. Wanna see?"

"Not now," I told him.

Kai looked towards the other end of the tent. "I have to go. My mom wants me. Nice meeting you, Gideon," she said. "See you later." Giving me a smile, she walked to her mom.

Once Kai was gone, Gideon grimaced. "Pain medicine is wearing off," he said. "I'm so sore. He took a deep breath, then winced. "Breathing too big makes my ribs move too much. She's pretty."

"Yes, she is."

"So, what have you been doing?" he asked.

The cloud I was riding evaporated. "Stopping trains," I answered. I felt as though I had crashed back to reality. "Look, Gideon, I am so sorry."

"For what?" he asked.

"For the cracked ribs," I said.

"A small price to pay for one's freedom," said a deep voice.

Masters walked over to the bed, carrying a tray. Smiling at us, he placed the tray on the tiny side table.

"Medicine time," he said. Masters handed Gideon a small cup full of liquid. While Gideon drank, Masters continued, "Gideon has been telling me about all that has happened." Taking the cup, he handed Gideon a glass. "Liquid nutrients.

Xavier Kelton, I sincerely thank you for being the catalyst that has freed us both. My name is Gideon Masters."

Shaking his hand, I looked from Masters to Gideon who was drinking his dinner.

"Yes, Gideon is my son," Masters said proudly. "My wife was pregnant when I went away. All these years not knowing. All I knew is if it were a boy, he would be named Gideon, after me, a girl would have been named Lucinda, after my wife." He took the empty glass from Gideon. "We have a lot of catching up to do." Looking at his son, Masters' hardness softened. "Because of you, this is possible. Don't feel badly about a few cracked ribs, Xavier. They'll heal quickly."

"Rover heading towards camp!" someone yelled.

My stomach dropped. Masters pulled out his gun, then nodded for me to go.

Outside, people ran every which way like they had battle stations.

Meeting Jett, I asked, "How many are there?"

"One."

"Only one? Are you sure?" I was confused.

"Look," he pointed.

Beyond the tents, the rover stayed at a safe distance. When it stopped, two figures emerged with their hands high in the air. Leaving the rover, they walked towards the camp. Lightning flashed across the sky illuminating their faces.

"Douglas! Thane!" I yelled.

Running to the camp entrance, I said, "It's Douglas!"

"Not so fast," said Char.

"But it's Douglas with a friend of mine," I told her.

Char stood with a large gun ready. "No buts," she said. "Douglas knows the rules. We shoot first; ask questions later."

With their arms still raised, Douglas and Thane walked slowly across the field. Even the lightning and thunder did not cause them to stray. As I waited, large raindrops crashed into everything.

Once they reached the camp, only Char lowered her weapon.

"About time," Char said to Douglas as if he were late for dinner. "Friend of yours?"

"You know how I like making new friends," quipped Douglas.

Char addressed Jett and me, "Take them to the tent."

Accompanying Douglas made me feel better about leaving him.

"What happened to you?" I asked.

"Tough bear," said Douglas. "Thankfully, he was a good laser shield. The gunshots drew them into the woods. When some lights blew, more came. Thane, here, interrupted our shootout. Drove the rover between me and the Units. Figured he was crazy. When he started shooting them, I got in. They retreated, but it's only a matter of time."

When we entered the tent, Douglas said to Exie, "They don't like us much."

"Tell us something we don't know," said Exie.

"They will find another way to get to Capital City and mow us all down in the process," Thane said. "Whatever you're planning, it better be post haste."

Exie looked Thane over once, then focused her attention on

Char who entered after us. "Gather everyone who can use a gun," she said to Char. "We'll meet you out there."

With a sharp nod, Char left.

"We have three divisions," Exie said. "Commander Gregory and his circle need to be neutralized. The Protector Units need a distraction. And, this camp needs to be defended."

"Excuse me," said Masters, cautiously entering the tent. "Xavier, Gideon said that you might need what is in here." He extended Gideon's bag towards me.

Looking at his bag, I realized he had spare parts from the Electric Commission. "Thanks, Mister Masters," I said.

"Mister," his deep voiced repeated like it was a foreign word.

"Been a long time, Lieutenant," said Thane. "Think you still know how Commander Gregory operates his inner circle?"

Masters breathed so hard through his nose, flames could have escaped. "You mean other than framing a man for murder, jailing his wife, and forcing his son to be a second class citizen?" His dark eyes narrowed. "Everyday, for thirteen years, I would mentally go through that complex and plan how to take out every last son of a," the last word did not escape his gritted teeth. His fists clenched tightly.

"You're in the hunting party, Lieutenant Masters," said Exie. "Welcome. I'm the General of this little operation."

Masters relinquished the bag to me while Exie barked orders.

"Also with me in the hunting party are Douglas, Char, and Xavier." Looking at me, she said, "We're going to need you to open doors."

I nodded.

"Jett, Mazie, you will lead the general force with the assistance of Caleb, Sadie, and the new guy," Exie continued. "Take with you as many who know the city layout as possible."

"What about me?" said Nickie.

"You're the director of base operations," Exie explained. "Brayden, you're in charge of defense."

"But you are all leaving me without anything," said Nickie. Her light eyes pleaded with us not to go.

Mom took Nickie's hand. "Your father and I will come back for you, Nickie. So will Xavier. That is a promise. All we want is a better life for you. We must do whatever it takes. Okay?"

Nickie nodded.

Gathering my bag, I brought them both to the table. Opening them, I began to scatter all the spare parts across the table. In Gideon's bag, I found a portable welding set and his laser proof vest.

Handing the vest to Dad, I asked, "Does it still work?"

Dad examined it. "Yes. Getting hit like that did not damage it," he said proudly. Giving it to Nickie, he added, "A laser proof vest for your protection."

Her fingers caressed the dark cloth. "Jett," she said, "you need this more than I."

While Jett smiled at Nickie, I began to construct a monitoring device out of the spare parts.

"You come back, too," Nickie said softly.

"Only for you," he whispered.

When I looked up, Jett was pulling the vest over his body.

"Here," I said, pushing the small box across the table to Nickie. "This will receive the same low frequency the scrollpads are emitting. You'll know our every move."

Nickie looked relieved. "Thanks, Xav. Be careful."

"Can I make something out of these?" Brayden asked me.

"Sure," I answered. "Brought them back in case you needed them."

Exie took one last look around before saying, "Let's go meet the troops."

Chapter 27

In an empty area by the weapons tent, Char had gathered many people, young and old.

"There are two important jobs for which you can volunteer," Exie addressed the crowd. "Defend the camp and attack PC one-five. Those who wish to join the attack will follow Jett and Mazie inside the tent where you will be assigned two weapons—a primary and a secondary. Those who wish to defend will get your weapons and posts from Brayden. After you get your weapons, line up out here."

When the people began to move, Exie said quietly, "Caleb, would you be able to go over the finer points of laser guns?"

Dad shook his head. "Thane's the better man for the job. He's the expert."

She looked at Thane in his blue Protector's uniform.

"Gregory gave the order to kill his wife in the Health Commission with innocent onlookers," Dad told her. "That same day, his three year old was lethally injected. Grief was the only reason why he did not lash out right away. Since their deaths, all he tried to do was save people."

Nodding, Exie approached Thane.

I followed Mom and Dad into the tent. Hanging back a little, I allowed others to get their weapons first.

"Lucinda," I heard Masters' deep voice say, "is that you?"

"Gideon?" said a woman's voice.

Out of the corner of my eye, I saw Masters hug a petite woman with long black braids.

"Lucinda, I thought I'd never see you again," said Masters. "Gideon said you were dead."

Lucinda placed a hand over her mouth. "You've met him?"

"He is the spitting image of you," said Masters.

"I always thought that he looked just like you," she said. "Where is he? Is he safe?"

"He's fine. He's in the medical tent with cracked ribs," Masters comforted.

Tears streamed down Lucinda's face. "Oh, my baby, my baby," she cried as she collapsed into Masters' arms. "I've been trying to get him out for years. All the reconnaissance I've done has been unsuccessful. I need to see him, be with him." She collected herself. "Are you going after Gregory?"

"I am."

"I was going to go search for Gideon and you when we stormed PC one-five. Now, I'll be defending our little Gideon," she said. "You give Gregory everything he deserves and then some."

With a gentleness unbefitting such a large man, Masters wiped any remaining tears from Lucinda's cheeks. "He'll get what's coming to him, darling." Gazing into her eyes, he said, "I love you, Luce. Always have, always will."

"I love you too, Gid," she said.

When they kissed, I realized how many lives were destroyed by the Pod City system. Taking them down was our only option.

"Xavier," said Douglas, interrupting my thoughts, "do you still have that handgun Jett gave you?"

"Yes," I replied.

"Good. Take this." He handed me a long black gun with two handles and a shoulder strap.

Looking at the gargantuan gun in my hands, I said, "I don't know how to use this."

"Don't worry about that," he said. "I'm not expecting you to use it. Just carry it."

Before I could say anything else, Douglas was securing the gun across my back. I was beginning to feel stupid until I saw that Jett looked just like me.

Outside, the rain tapped our heads. Once everyone had assembled, Thane discussed laser guns.

"Lasers are invisible and when the guns are set to stun, they are also silent," explained Thane. "However, when you look directly at a laser gun's barrel, you can see a white light twinkle as the internal mirror rotates. When the laser gun is set on kill, you can hear it power up seconds before the laser leaves the gun. It gives you a split second to avoid the fatal beam."

"Thank you, Thane," said Exie. "Our only real defense is guerilla style warfare. Do what you need to do to protect yourself and each other. Either they surrender or they die. They have tried long and hard to destroy us—the people. Like the wise men before us, let us pledge to each other our sacred honors so that we and those who come after can live in a better world free of this tyranny and without exile. Let's fight for our families, our future, and our freedom."

Everyone who heard her battle cry responded with a cheer. The cold rain could not dampen the fighting spirit.

Jett and I followed Exie out of the camp. Before we reached the rover that Douglas and Thane left, Exie told us, "Keep a tree between you and PC one-five as we approach."

With a sharp nod of good luck, Jett separated from the hunting party. He collected a small team of people to follow him. Mom, Dad, and Mazie did the same. I walked closer to Douglas and Masters.

"Whose murder?" Douglas asked Masters.

"Tinsey Ambers," Masters replied. "I was selected to protect the Commandant and his new wife. One night, Richard Ambers runs into the Protectors' quarters, screaming that his wife was gone from their bed. After the house and grounds were searched, Commander Gregory was called in to supervise the wilderness search. As Lieutenant of the Commandant's Protector Unit, I was chosen to go with Gregory's team. He told us to keep our guns drawn.

"It was nearing daybreak when we heard a woman crying. 'Misses Ambers,' I called out to her, 'it's Lieutenant Masters.' She cried even more.

"'No, don't come. I don't want…,' was the last thing I heard her say. By the time I reached her, she was dead. One of Gregory's team shot her. I can still remember how sad she looked. Her light red hair was wet with tears. Her nightgown was torn and dirty. She wasn't even wearing shoes. At that moment, I knew something was wrong. I never thought that I would have been accused, then found guilty, of her murder."

"How did they not execute you?" asked Douglas.

"Gregory pushed hard for it," Masters said. "But the labor camp needed strong bodies to work either in the mines, the mills, or in the power plants. Gregory was overruled. Ambers couldn't have cared less. I heard he inherited his wife's Globals and continued to surround himself with exotic items and young boys. He and Gregory conspired to kill Tinsey. I wouldn't be surprised if Gregory pulled the trigger himself."

Reaching the trees, Exie ordered, "Total silence from this point forward."

Douglas motioned for me to pull the hat over my face. Wiping off the rain, I followed instructions.

We were like marauders creeping through the forest. In the rain, we tiptoed from tree to tree. The attack teams spread out around us.

The strobing lights from PC one-five made it feel as though we weren't really moving. With the fence in sight, Exie crouched next to me.

"How's it look?" she whispered.

Pulling out my scrollpad, I ran a city diagnostic. "Most of the city has short circuited," I whispered. "The Electric Commission is dark, so there is no chance of real repair. The fence and its weapons have burned. A backup system is keeping part of the Protector Complex up and running."

"Can you disable it?"

"Not from here. It must be a self-contained system. I have no control over it. Hardwiring would be the only way."

"We'll get you control," she assured me. "Can we enter?"

"With ease," I told Exie.

Leaving me, Exie moved to the front with her arm over her head in a chopping motion. People carrying large wire cutters ran towards the fence. We weren't all going to enter through the front gate.

Thunder masked the clanging of the chain link fence being cut. But, no matter how vigorously the thunder clapped, it could not cover the sound of the first gunshot.

Wood splintered around me. My heart raced madly. I had not signed up for this. Or had I? All I wanted was my family back. The family *they* took from me.

"Time to move," yelled Douglas.

"Stay close, Kid," said Char.

Leaving our positions, we charged the front gate. Protectors scrambled. Many of them dropped. I saw some on our side drop, too. Who was it? Mom? Dad? Mazie? Jett? Thane?

Douglas pulled me inside an opened door. "It's hard to see your fellow men fall," he told me. "We have a job to do. Let that be your focus. And let them do their jobs, too. You can't do both. Now, follow Masters."

Nodding, I followed Masters down a narrow, white hallway. The lights sort of worked. Every now and then, something sparked. Douglas and Char followed me, making sure no one caught us from behind. Masters gave Exie directions while I observed the battle on my scrollpad.

Mazie set off explosives that rocked the building I wandered. Mom led her team around the outer complexes. With a gun in each hand, the Protectors never saw her coming. Dad's team secured perches. They defended those on the ground. Regular citizens poached weapons off the fallen and joined the fight. Around the fence, Jett's team found posts so that no one could escape.

As I scrolled through the cameras, the only one I could not find was Thane. Had he fallen? Or was he simply a loose cannon?

My body slammed into the wall when a shot echoed in the narrow hallway. Douglas' arm pinned me in place while Exie shot Protectors.

When the shooting stopped, Exie said, "Well, they know we're here."

We crawled further inside the complex. The sounds of the battle outside no longer reached our ears. I stopped checking my scrollpad for updates, fearing an ambush. Every time the scroll-pad opened a door, I expected a fight. We all did. But, every time, no one was there.

"I don't like this," said Douglas.

"Neither do I," Masters agreed. "There should be guards at every checkpoint before we reach the brain room. Its door is down the corridor to the right."

Searching the working camera feeds inside the complex, I said, "Exie, wait."

She turned.

"That corridor is brighter than the others," I told her. "It's beyond my control."

Nodding, Exie said, "Then cameras and a secure door are our obstacles."

"I should be able to crack the door, but they'll see us," I said. "And, they'll know exactly who I am." Looking at my scrollpad, I remembered Commander Gregory returning it to me. "Let me try something." Getting out of the camera feeds, I loaded my paranoia program.

My scrollpad scanned for devices. "There are no less than four thermal cameras and a matrix of laser sensors. The door has a keypad with a hand and retinal scanner."

"Do we shoot it up and flush them out?" asked Char.

"They'll expect that," Masters said.

"What was your plan?" said Char.

"Camouflage with the other Protectors as they entered," Masters answered.

As the scrollpad continued scanning, I saw our answer. "There's a service panel," I said. "But, I need to be in the hall in full view of the cameras."

"Time to put your father's technology to the ultimate test," said Douglas.

We had come this far. I was not going to let them down now. Extracting my screwdriver from my scrollpad, I took a deep breath. My heart pounded loudly as I tiptoed into the hall alone.

Using the scrollpad as my guide, I found the panel. It was well hidden. I scraped the screwdriver across the wall until it hit something. It hit two somethings. Carefully, I pried off plastic flaps that covered screws. Unscrewing them, the panel would not open. I scraped the wall some more. Finding the other two flaps, I had the panel off in no time.

Quickly, I hardwired my scrollpad into the system. Not wanting to be detected, I tricked the thermal cameras into not seeing heat signatures. Then, I redirected the power from the laser sensors so that they would slowly overload the system.

Removing my scrollpad from the wall, I tiptoed back to the hall crossing. After waving them forward, I made a beeline to the door's security pad.

The security pad had no screws either. Nor was it similar to any of the pads in the rest of the Pod City. Stumped, I stared at it. Then, Douglas held a large knife in front of my face.

Slipping the blade between the wall and the panel, I began to pry. With a little persuasion and lots of prying, the security pad popped off the wall. It dangled from a wiring mess. I used the tip of the knife to follow the wires. Putting away my scrollpad, I pulled a wire out of the wall as far as it would stretch. Douglas' sharp blade cleanly cut through the wire. The door slid open.

Guns drawn, we stepped through the door. An empty, wide hallway greeted us. Exie looked at me imploringly.

Everyone waited as my scrollpad scanned.

Looking at Exie, I shook my head.

"Nothing?" she said.

"Unless I can't see it."

Raising her eyebrows, she said, "So much for technology. We do this the old-fashioned way. Shoot anything that moves."

Like a siren singing her song, the deserted hallways lured us deeper into the unknown. Nothing moved between the smooth white walls but us. Around every turn, no one waited.

Exie raised her fist for us to stop. "Listen," she whispered.

I lifted my hat away from my ear. A strange, singing like hum waltzed from someplace up ahead.

For the first time, fear flickered across Douglas' face. "What do you suppose that is?" he asked.

"I don't know, but I think we'll find out soon enough," said Exie.

The further we crept, the more prominent the hum became. Eventually, we reached a door that rattled to the singing hum. Beside the door, there was no keypad, no biometric scanner, no voice recognition device, only bare wall. The door had a single round doorknob.

Scanning the area, there seemed to be no security or electrical devices of any kind. Still, Douglas insisted that he open the door with his special gloved hand while the rest of us readied to shoot.

Turning the knob, the door swung into a large room. Again, we faced no one. Before we crossed the threshold, Exie had me scan the room.

My screen flashed. "I can't get a proper reading," I said. "There is so much electrical activity it is overloading my scroll-pad."

Exie swallowed hard. "Expect the worst," she said.

Tucking my scrollpad into my pocket, I stepped over the threshold with them. The room was ten times bigger than the generator room in the bunker system. An eerie glow illuminated the dark corners of the room. In the center, I found the source of the glow.

A massive machine filled the room, reaching from floor to

ceiling. A weird glow emitted from what looked like a surrounding force field. Behind the force field, the machine looked to be devouring colored rocks.

"Sounds like a bunch of tuning forks," said Masters, staring at it.

"Are those gemstones?" Char asked.

"They're using them as an energy source," said Douglas. "Very controversial."

He took another step closer. A sharp buzz replaced the humming. Douglas jumped backwards.

Different colored laser beams shot from everywhere. Scrambling, we retreated to the door.

As we stood in the doorway, we watched the lasers search for us.

"We need to shut that down," said Exie.

"Controls would be on the opposite side of the room if not in another room," I said.

"Which requires crossing the room," said Masters.

Char studied the room from the threshold. "Xavier, give me the gun on your back," she said.

After lifting the strap over my head, I handed it to her. In return, she gave me her handgun.

"What are you thinking?" Exie asked Char.

"Gotta take out the lasers," Char answered. "Xavier, you get to the other side and shut this thing down."

"That's suicide," exclaimed Douglas.

Determined, she said, "Take good care of her, Doug."

Char stepped away from us. Rapid gunfire joined the buzzing.

"Go!" yelled Exie.

Dodging lasers, I heard even more rapid gunfire as I ran around the gemstone munching generator. On the other side of the room, I found the control center.

A large screen was integrated into the back wall. Next to the screen was a plastic panel. Flipping it open, I found switches and circuits. To expose the wires, I popped off the plastic circuit switches. With my screwdriver in hand, I tried to shut out the sounds around me while I wired my scrollpad to the circuit board.

I was in the middle of wiring when something hard tapped the back of my head.

"Hello again, Xavier," said a man's voice in my ear. "Hand me the scrollpad and I won't fry your brains."

"Only for you to kill me after I give it you?" I said. "The technology you want won't work if I'm dead."

He removed the gun from my head.

I caught a glimpse of his highly decorated Protector uniform. Mister Many Bars—Commander Gregory—was hiding in the generator room while his Units died outside.

His arm wrapped around my neck. "You're nothing but a punk kid who had talented, yet defiant, parents," Gregory said with anger.

He squeezed. My throat closed. I gasped for breath. My hands tried to pry his arm away from my neck. I still held onto my screwdriver.

Gripping the handle tightly, my arm swung downwards. The screwdriver point dug into flesh. I poked upwards inside his leg. Commander Gregory let go of me.

He stumbled backwards with the screwdriver in his thigh. Grabbing his gun, Commander Gregory fell to the ground.

Looking through where he once stood, I saw Thane with a gun pointed at Gregory's lifeless form.

Thane disappeared into the smoke encompassed room. With a hole in his head, Commander Gregory could not assault me again.

Returning to the circuit board, my scrollpad was gone. Frantically, I searched. In the spark ridden smoke, I could not find it.

As I ran to the large screen, someone grabbed my arms. As they were pinned behind me, I heard a male voice say one word, "Walk."

My feet moved, one in front of the other. The only thing I knew about my kidnapper was that he was strong.

He pushed me through another door into another hall. With a strong hand's hard yank, my hat covered my eyes, eclipsing the bright light.

I squirmed. A gun fired.

The man groaned in my ear.

Something covered my nose and mouth. A pungent, chemical-y odor infiltrated my nostrils.

Chapter 28

My wrists hurt. Slowly, my eyelids opened. A room full of tables and shelves came into focus. On one of the tables, my guns laid. One was in pieces. My scrollpad sat open on another table. Looking around, I noticed my feet bound with chains. Above my head, chains held my wrists.

Across the room, a door opened. A burly man with a slight limp and a blood stained pant leg approached me.

"About time you woke," he said. "So, you're the infamous Xavier Kelton. If Gregory and Ambers could have done one simple task, I wouldn't have to be here. Yet, here I am. And, here you are."

"Who are you?" I asked.

"You know, if you weren't such a problem, I would want to

have you on my team in Capital City. I'm Protector General Oliver Sutton."

"What do you want with me? Shouldn't you be protecting the President?"

He laughed. "That moron?" he said, laughing again. "Easily replaceable. The President is nothing but a puppet like his mother and grandfather were before him and his children and grandchildren will be after him. *I*," he said, pointing to his chest, "am the puppet master. *I* pull all the strings. If it happens in this country, it is because *I* made it so."

Sutton limped to a table. Picking up my scrollpad, he said, "This even stumped the late Doctor Young. Nanolife was genius. It brought a special uncertainty to life. Shame that it's gone, but there will be other ways."

The man was sick. I had to avert my eyes as he fondled my scrollpad.

"Tell me," he began. "Look at me when I'm talking to you, Boy!"

Unfortunately, my eyes found him still holding my scrollpad.

"Is it DNA based?"

"You'd have to ask my mom," I said.

He placed it on the table with the guns. As he strolled towards some contraption I had not seen, he said, "Wrong answer, Xavier."

The whole room shook or my body convulsed. Burning raced right under my skin.

Once I had stopped shaking, Sutton held his face close to mine. "Don't you just love highly conductive metals? They allow electricity to flow so effortlessly. Then, there's the human body. Full of all that water." He smiled.

"Now," he said, backing away from me, "let's try this again. Shall we? How does it work?"

"My parents collaborated on what they called nanotouch technology," I answered.

"And?"

"It is only receptive to the person or persons for whom it has been tailored."

"How come we haven't been able to duplicate it?" asked Sutton.

"I don't know."

Fire burned through my body again.

"Does it feel better to let out a good scream?" he taunted.

I did not know I had screamed.

"Why can it not be replicated?" he asked.

"It needs a key," I said.

He got in my face again. "What kind of key?"

"The individual's electronic signature."

Taking a few steps back, he asked, "What is that?"

"It's like a fingerprint or DNA. Each person produces small amounts of electricity in the brain, which travels through the body before returning to the brain. The pattern it creates in our bodies is different for each person. But, unlike fingerprints or DNA, a person's electronic signature disappears at death," I explained.

Sutton's forehead wrinkled. "Convenient. So, I can't kill you... yet."

Grabbing the scrollpad, he thrust it into my bound hands. Then, he disappeared behind the shelves. My hands could barely feel the thin plastic. I heard scraping and shuffling noises as if Sutton was searching for something.

The lights went out. Sutton swore. The scrollpad slipped out of my fingers. Plastic crashed beneath my feet. Heavy footsteps crossed the room.

A boom shook me in my chains. Through smoke, passing light shone in my face. For a fleeting momement, I saw the door lying on top of Sutton.

"Xavier!" Nickie's voice called to me.

I heard two gunshots, then I fell to the floor. Standing, plastic crunched under my foot.

Nickie pointed the flashlight on my feet. My scrollpad was nothing but scattered broken gray plastic and wires.

"I'm sorry," she said.

"It doesn't matter," I told her. "Let's go."

"Not so fast," Sutton said. He walked near the light, holding my gun at us. "You're both coming with me. You need to fix what you broke."

I put a reassuring hand on Nickie's back. My hand touched a hard, pebbly sphere. Pulling it from its holder, my finger removed the pin.

When the pin clinked on the ground, Nickie shut off the flashlight and I threw the grenade. We scrambled behind the shelves before the explosion.

I heard, *bang, bang, bang.* Turning on the flashlight, we saw the shelves falling towards us. We crawled to safety.

Quickly scanning the room with the light, we found the opening. I took her hand, then we ran.

In the hall, I could hear muffled screaming and banging. Like a pendulum, the light swung from wall to wall. Nickie and I scurried as we searched for the source.

From behind a door, I heard Masters' deep voice, asking, "Is anyone out there?"

Nickie knocked twice. The banging and yelling stopped. "Stand back!" she said.

She handed me her gun and flashlight. Removing a grenade from her belt, she placed it in front of the door. We backed away, covered our ears, and turned.

After the explosion, she took the flashlight from me. Pouring light into the room, we found Masters, Exie, Douglas, Thane, and Char.

"What happened?" I asked.

"Ambush," said Exie. "We were knocked out by some sort of gas. Woke up in here."

"Why did the lights go out?" asked Douglas.

"Brayden modified a laser gun with the parts that Xavier brought into an EMP gun," Nickie said.

Thane held Char in his arms. "She needs a doctor," he said.

Gazing at Char, Nickie nodded. "This way."

We started to walk back the way we came when the distinct sound of a gunshot echoed in the hall. I felt something graze my arm before it hit the wall behind me.

Nickie shined the light in the direction of the shot. Protector General Sutton held himself up against the wall.

With the only gun between us in my hands, I shot.

Sutton slid down the wall. He lifted the gun.

Without hesitation, I shot twice.

Nothing moved.

Taking the gun from me, Douglas approached Sutton's body. He placed fingers against his neck. "He's dead," Douglas said.

We followed Nickie towards Douglas as he relieved the body of the gun.

Douglas handed me back the gun, saying, "Good job, Xavier." Grabbing my arm, he said, "Looks like a bullet nicked you. Don't worry, it's just a scratch."

As we walked, I asked Nickie, "How'd you find us?"

"I used the receiver you made," said Nickie as though it were obvious. "And, then followed the trail of blood, hoping that it wasn't one of you." Shining the flashlight on the floor, dark red spotted the light floor.

"I inadvertently shot the Protector General in the leg," I said.

"Served him right," Masters muttered.

The generator room greeted us with silence. Masters and Exie collected forgotten weapons off the floor. Crossing the room, the light scanned scattered bodies of Protectors.

We retraced our steps through the complex. Nickie's flashlight was our only light source. Everything electrical was dead.

Outside, early morning rays poked through the clouds. The Redux Radix patrolled makeshift prisons. Fires warmed the brisk morning air. The wounded were being tended.

Dad greeted us. He brought us to Mom, Mazie, and Jett. While Mom cleaned my arm, I heard Mazie cry, "Char!

"Mazie," Char could barely speak. "We've had a great run. Be happy with Douglas."

Tears streamed down Mazie's cheeks. "This is not goodbye!"

"You've been a great friend," said Char.

"We still are. And we'll always be great friends," Mazie sobbed.

"Danny's waiting for me."

"No! He can wait longer," Mazie said defiantly.

Masters drove a rover to Thane and Char. "They won't be able to do anything for her here," said Masters.

Dad opened the back of the rover. As Thane laid Char delicately inside, Dad told Mazie, "I'll be with her."

Douglas tried to hold Mazie upright while she cried uncontrollably.

"We'll send word," Mom softly said to Mazie.

Mazie nodded.

"Take this," said Exie, handing Mom a dark blue triangle. "Fly it out of the rover when you get near the camp so they don't shoot you." Sadly, she looked at Char. "Bring it back when, you know."

"Get in, kids," Mom told us.

Dad got in the front with Masters while the three of us climbed in the back with Thane and Char. Mom hugged the blue triangle tightly as Masters drove the rover away from PC one-five.

"You look good, Danny," Char breathed. She gazed at a spot somewhere on the back of the rover.

"Who's Danny?" asked Thane.

"My fiancé," Char answered with a smile on her face.

"Isn't that nice that he came to see how you're doing," said Thane.

"Yeah."

"I bet you he's socializing with my wife, Eliza, and my son,

George," Thane said with glossy eyes. "They're waiting for me, you know."

"Like my Danny."

"Yes, but they're going to be waiting for a long time. So they can keep watch over Danny while he waits for you."

Char turned her eyes towards Thane.

"Danny would want you to stay with us for a little while. He's in no rush," Thane told her.

"Camp in sight," said Dad.

Mom unfolded the blue triangle, then handed it to Dad. The rushing wind caught it as Dad held it out the window. I could see red and white flash every so often. As we approached the camp, we could hear cheering. They knew it was over.

Brayden met the rover when Masters parked as close as possible. Dad quickly opened the back. Glancing at Char, Brayden's expression changed from elated to concerned.

No one said a word as Thane scooped her out of the rover. We processed behind Thane carrying Char to the medical tent.

Entering the tent, Brayden screamed, "Phoebe!"

Doctor Meltac came running. She took one look at Char, then said, "I need the gurney!"

Nurses brought a bed on wheels onto which Char was carefully placed. Doctor Meltac helped roll Char into what looked like an adjoining tent.

Kai crept over with worry in her bright blue eyes. "What happened?"

"She sacrificed herself," I answered.

Placing a hand over her mouth, Kai closed her eyes for a moment. "What happened to your arm?" she asked.

"I was shot."

"Xavier," said Mom, "you should have it checked and medicine put on it. We'll be in the command tent."

Kai had me sit on an empty bed while she removed the bandage. They all left the tent except Masters. He walked over to Gideon's bed where his wife greeted him with a hug.

"You have to take the shirt off," Kai instructed. "The material is so tough I'm afraid that I would cut you trying to open the hole."

I peeled both the vest and shirt off together. As I put them beside me, I thought I caught Kai blush.

She poured something on a small ball. "This may sting," warned Kai before dabbing my arm.

It did sting, but I wasn't going to tell her.

With a small flat stick, she applied a thick gel over the wound. "This is so it doesn't get infected," she explained when she caught me watching.

Gently, Kai taped on a bandage.

"Thanks," I said.

"You're welcome. You can put your shirt back on now."

After pulling the shirt over my head, Kai sat down next to me on the bed.

"Were you scared?" she asked quietly.

"Initially," I admitted. "Then, adrenaline took over, I think. Fear returned after being electrocuted the second time."

"That's horrible," she said, placing her hand on mine.

Turning my palm to meet hers, I squeezed.

"What was it like here?" I asked.

"A lot of nervous waiting," answered Kai. "Until we saw

you guys bring the flag. Then we knew it was over."

"Can you come with me to the other tent?" I asked.

Nodding, Kai said, "There's nothing left for me to do here. I'm allowed to dress wounds, but I can't assist with surgery."

As we stood, Gideon called, "Xavier! Come here."

I tugged on Kai's arm to let her know that she could come, too.

"Xavier, I want you to meet my mom," said Gideon. He smiled widely when he said *mom*.

"It is nice to meet you, Missus Masters," I said.

She answered with a bone crushing hug. "Thank you for my son and my husband," she said. Letting go, she looked at me, saying, "I don't know how we can ever repay you."

I shook my head. "You're together. That's what counts."

While we walked in between tents, I caught Kai's hand in mine. She made the worry about Char more bearable.

We dropped hands before entering the command tent. Inside, I introduced Kai to Mom.

"You're Doctor Meltac's daughter," Mom said.

"Yes, I am," Kai answered.

"And do you want to follow in your mother's footsteps?" asked Mom.

"I think so," Kai said with a smile.

Pleasant conversation could only last so long. I sat at the table with Nickie and Kai. The others sometimes sat, sometimes paced. The waiting was excruciating. I did not want to imagine what Mazie was going through back in the Pod City.

After what seemed like an eternity, Doctor Meltac walked through the tent opening. Everyone stopped to hear her.

"She's lost a lot of blood, but she's stable," said Doctor Meltac. "Char will recover, in time."

The entire tent sighed in relief.

"When she's strong enough, I'd like to move her to my hospital," Doctor Meltac added. "In a rover perhaps?"

"I will drive," said Thane.

"We should get back to Mazie and Exie," Dad said. "Thanks, Phoebe."

"Mom," said Kai, "can I go?"

She smiled at her daughter. "As long as you stay with the Keltons," Doctor Meltac said.

Kai hugged her. "Thanks, Mom."

Thane and Brayden stayed in the tent as the five of us returned to the rover. Mom and Dad got in the front while Nickie, Kai, and I jumped in the back.

When Dad started the rover, Mom asked, "Do you remember how to drive?"

"It's only been about twenty-five or so years," Dad said. "Shouldn't be too hard."

They laughed. Nickie and I smiled at each other. It was good to hear our parents laugh again.

Dad was not the smooth driver that Masters was. We each found something to hold, stopping us from being tossed into each other. Driving through the gates of PC one-five, our bumpy ride ended where Exie waited.

When we got out of the rover, Mom handed Exie the flag she gave us. Dad gave Mazie the good news about Char to which she cried even more.

"Wow, look at this place," Kai said under her breath. She

gawked at the destruction riddled Pod City with awe.

Before we strayed too far, Exie called for everyone to follow her to the common area's flagpole. She held the flag over her head for all to see. The flag comprised of red and white stripes and white stars in a field of blue in the one corner.

"This has been known as 'Old Glory.' The flag of what once was the United States of America," Exie began. "We used to be a Federal Democratic Republic with each state having its own sovereignty and own constitution. It was a country where government's power was limited by a sole document of law—the Constitution. This document ensured its citizens liberty. Somewhere along the way, this document was ignored, shunted, and eventually, destroyed. Today is the first day towards the reinstatement of our original Constitution, towards having the liberty to lead the lives we choose."

As Exie brought the flag to the flagpole, she continued, "This flag may be old with its fifty stars, one for each state, but its meaning has not wavered—one people, united." Securing the flag, she began to pull the rope. "As I raise this flag, let it remind you of our resilience. This country can be great again. All it takes is we, the people."

While I watched the flag blow in the wind, I took Kai's hand in mine. The red, white, and blue shone brightly in the sunlight. Looking around, some of the older generations held their hands over their hearts. People sang songs I did not know. The songs sounded patriotic. I stood in the grass not knowing what the future held, but I knew it was mine.

Epilogue

Over the months that followed, Mom, Dad, Nickie, and I moved into great-grandma's big white farm-house that Nickie and I once took refuge in from the rain. Mazie and Douglas helped us restore it. They married in our backyard while the wildflowers were in full bloom.

Thane and Char became good friends. He helped her through a difficult rehabilitation. She was able to go from a wheelchair to walking with a cane.

With Whitetail's training, Jett found his parents. His aunt had leaked their whereabouts to the Pod Cities. Mister and Mrs. Barto had been captured to work in a Pod City's labor camp in another part of the country. He brought them home just in time to register for the special election.

We, the people, voted for a return to a Federal Republic of

states and commonwealths. Most of the original state borders and names returned. So did all the old city names. New government officials were elected on both the state and federal levels. Exie was voted in as President.

When Capital City—Washington, D.C.—fell, we cracked the secret database. Files showed who did what and when during our country's dark history. Many from the Pod City system were charged with treason. After a jury found them guilty, the treacherous were sent to rot in prison.

Power grids were restored across the country. Citizens settled in redesigned cities, formerly abandoned small towns, and forgotten rural areas. Midsummer, Mazie and Douglas, Char and Thane, Kai and her mother, Jett and his parents, and Gideon and his parents joined us at the farmhouse to watch the fireworks as the United States of America celebrated her Tricentennial.

About the Author

IE Castellano is an American author and poet living in the Eastern United States. Falling in love with the mechanics of the English language at an early age, she started writing poetry before venturing into fiction. She loves history (especially ancient), mythology, archeology, and anthropology. Anything IE reads, sees or does could wind up in one of her books in some manner. With her propensity to ask, what if, she writes speculative fiction—authoring the dystopian sci-fi novel, *Tricentennial*, and the contemporary epic fantasy series, *the World In-between*.

For news and a current list of her writings, visit her blog: IECastellano.blogspot.com. Contact IE at IECastellano@zoho.com.

Also by IE Castellano:
  The World In-between (The World In-between, 1)
  Bow of the Moon (The World In-between, 2)
  Secrets of the Sages (The World In-between, 3)
  Where Pirates Go to Die
  The Hunt (Moon Shadows)
  Yuletide Magic (A World In-between Short Story)

www.ingramcontent.com/pod-product-compliance
Lightning Source LLC
Chambersburg PA
CBHW050411260626
47156CB00003B/961